"I would [...] *you paid me.* [...] *Communists,"* Chesty sneered.

A shiver shook David's body. He blinked, took a breath, and glanced cautiously from Dillon to Reece and Van Kelt. They couldn't all agree with Chesty. They were too smart. They had to know better.

Van Kelt spit a mouthful of water into the sink. "And that's just the faculty," he said.

"What do I care how many Jews are at Harvard?" Dillon shrugged. "They're not in the clubs. You don't have to room with them. It's just like Princeton. You don't have to be around them if you don't want to."

David's heart was pounding so loudly he was surprised that no one else could hear it. He had to swallow hard to get rid of the lump in his throat before he could speak. "How would you ever know?" he asked.

"What?"

"If you were with . . . them."

"Are you kidding?" Dillon replied. "How would you *not* know? It's kinda hard to miss a hebe."

One by one the other boys drifted out of the bathroom. David contemplated his reflection in the mirror. He didn't owe anyone any explanations. And in the end he would have the last laugh, because Dillon, Van Kelt, and the rest would never know—unless he chose to tell them—that a dreaded Jew was moving among them. . . .

School ties

A Novel by
Deborah Chiel

Based on a Story by
Dick Wolf

Screenplay by
Dick Wolf and **Darryl Ponicsan**

POCKET BOOKS

New York   London   Toronto   Sydney   Tokyo   Singapore

An *Original* Publication of POCKET BOOKS

POCKET BOOKS, a division of Simon & Schuster Inc.
1230 Avenue of the Americas, New York, NY 10020

This book is published by Pocket Books, a division of Simon & Schuster Inc., under exclusive license from Paramount Pictures.

ISBN: 0-671-77715-7

First Pocket Books printing September 1992

10 9 8 7 6 5 4 3 2 1

For Jesse Krotick

1

On a warm September Sunday David Greene cruised the deserted downtown streets of Scranton, Pennsylvania, in his father's five-year-old Ford convertible. He had the road to himself. The stores were shuttered and locked, the sidewalks deserted except for two old men who sat dozing on a bench in front of the bank.

Poor old geezers, thought David. Probably they were killing time before the matinee started at the Odeon, where *Davy Crockett* had opened just the week before. There wasn't much else to do in Scranton on a Sunday morning besides go to church.

At seventeen, David Greene already knew that small-town life wasn't all it was cracked up to be. Most of his friends had no greater ambition than to live out the rest of their lives in the same shabby four-block radius where they had grown up together, working at the same dead-end jobs as their fathers. David, however, had secret hopes for his future—hopes that took him far beyond the borders of his hometown.

Visiting his relatives in New York, David had caught a glimpse of another world, one that seemed to offer endless possibilities for happiness and success. His aunt and uncle lived in a house on a tree-lined street in Brooklyn that resembled similar streets in Scranton. But the previous winter, on the final chilly day of 1954, David and his cousins had boarded the subway and ventured forth onto the bustling streets of Manhattan. They had ice-skated in Central Park, ogled the dinosaurs at the Museum of Natural History, and explored the shops and cafés of Greenwich Village.

Hours before midnight they had welcomed in the new year at a restaurant in Chinatown. There, awkwardly wielding a pair of chopsticks, David had sampled dish after dish of the most delicious food he had ever tasted. The slip of paper inside his fortune cookie had predicted, "You will travel to exotic places and make many new friends."

Now, in just a few hours, he would be leaving town to study at a school in Massachusetts. He had been looking forward to this day since last February, when the letter from St. Matthew's Academy had arrived in the mail.

A wet, sticky late-winter snow had been falling that afternoon, and David's father was late getting home from work. David had stared at the envelope, which lay atop a pile of bills and circulars. The return address in the upper left-hand corner, someplace in Massachusetts David had never heard of, was engraved with fancy black lettering. The back flap was sealed with an impressive-looking crest. The letter, which had been handwritten on thick cream-colored stationery, was addressed to Mr. Alan Greene. But the letter actually concerned Mr. Greene's oldest son, David.

"They want to give you a full scholarship," his father announced with stunned wonderment in his voice. "They want you to play football for them, David. Do you understand what this means? They're offering you the opportunity of a lifetime!"

A series of phone calls had followed between the St. Matthew's principal, who was known as the headmaster; the coach, Mr. McDevitt; and the Greenes. It had seemed almost a foregone conclusion that David would attend St. Matthew's. His father obviously believed he would be crazy to decide otherwise. David thought so, too.

The school was his ticket out of Scranton. He fantasized about making new friends, being invited to their homes over the holidays, taking trips to New York, Boston, maybe even Washington or Chicago.

The news about his scholarship spread quickly at school. Some of the teachers congratulated him on his good fortune; others sternly remarked that he would have to work doubly hard until the end of the year in order to meet St. Matthew's tough academic standards. His closest friends were shocked to hear he was leaving. David was their star quarterback. How could he desert the team? Besides, except for the girls who got pregnant and were sent away to have their babies, or the guys who dropped out to go work in the mines, nobody ever left before graduation.

Although his buddies had finally gotten used to the idea, this morning, as David slowly cruised the street and mentally said good-bye to all his favorite haunts, he wondered whether he'd made a really dumb mistake. Maybe all small towns felt this dead and dull on Sunday mornings when most people were asleep or in church. Maybe he should have stuck around, finished off the year with his buddies, and gone on to play for Penn State. Maybe his father's assurances that he would fit in perfectly at St. Matthew's added up to nothing more than a blast of hot air.

He turned right at the service station, where the price of gas had just gone up to eighteen cents a gallon, and waved at his friend Kenny, whose father owned the place. Passing the movie house, he remembered the night this summer when Annette Zagourney had let him feel her up over her shirt.

Later he had driven her home and kissed her good-night at the door. "Write to me this year, okay?" she had whispered. He had said sure, he would write, and he meant it. But now, as Fats Domino wailed "Ain't That a Shame" on the car radio, David realized he had lied to Annette. She was a sweet girl, but he couldn't think about her when he was hundreds of miles from home, struggling to keep up with the other students at St. Matthew's Academy.

The church bells were pealing out a welcome to

the stream of worshipers filing through the front door of the Greek Orthodox church on the corner. Stopped at a red light in front of the church, David stared at the recently refurbished onion-shaped dome, sparkling in the sunshine. The dome had been hidden for many months behind a web of scaffolding while a team of workmen scrubbed away the layers of coal dust that had accumulated over the years.

The greasy black soot was a fact of life in Scranton, where the mines had dominated the economy for decades and brought waves of immigrants to the Lackawanna Valley. More recently coal production had been drastically cut, and many of the mines had been closed down. But still the dust, a gritty relic of a more prosperous period in the history of the area, hung in the air above the town.

It clung to the facades of the row houses that lined the blocks adjacent to the church, turning the brick from red to dull gray. Even in the bright morning light the houses looked drab and decrepit. Testifying to the former gentility of the neighborhood were the panes of leaded glass, now gone dingy with age, that had once glistened in the front doors of the houses. The potholes in the road further attested to the declining fortunes of the region.

Here and there an elderly woman sat rocking on the porch. This was a street of many widows, the wives of miners whose lungs had turned as black as the coal they had gouged out of the earth. Some of them David knew by name; his friend Bear's grandmother, Mrs. Yacek, for example, who waved at him as he swerved to avoid the crater-sized rut that would have destroyed the Ford's already weakened shocks. She was a nice lady who spoke with a thick Polish accent that reminded David of his grandfather.

The way Bear dug into his grandmother's plates of fried potato dumplings, kielbasa, and meat-stuffed cabbage, it was no wonder he was the powerhouse of the football team: a fierce fullback who moved downfield like a Mack truck, mowing down the opposing tacklers. David was sure going to miss Bear, whom he had met back in junior high school.

They had played touch football for hours at a stretch, practicing their moves on David's front lawn. David would call the plays, and Bear would tear across the balding, patchy grass to score a touchdown. By the time they both made the high school team they had already won a thousand imaginary games together.

With David as quarterback and Bear as tight end they had won a heck of a lot of real ones together, too. They had celebrated all the home game victories with Coke and greasy french fries doused in ketchup at Edie's Luncheonette, where David was headed now to say good-bye to the gang.

Edie's was kind of a dump. The walls looked as if they hadn't been painted since before the war, and generations of students had carved their initials into the wooden tabletops of the vinyl-backed booths. But it was the only place in the neighborhood where a guy could go and not feel like he had to be on his best behavior for the grownups.

He pulled into a parking space, checked himself in the rearview mirror, and ran his pocket comb through his dark brown hair. As usual, the curls wouldn't stay flat, no matter how much Brylcreem he used to slick them down, nor could he get the DA in back to lie exactly the way he wanted. On the other hand, he didn't have any major zits, and the shadow of mustache stubble proved he had already started shaving.

He wasn't the best-looking guy in the senior class, but he was no troll. Annette Zagourney said he looked like Rock Hudson. Though he would have preferred Marlon Brando or James Dean, whose pompadour and tight jeans he had adopted, he was flattered by the comparison.

He got out of the car, shrugged off the maroon corduroy sports jacket his dad had brought home for him yesterday, and nodded at the group of regulars who considered the ten or so feet on either side of Edie's Coke machine their own private turf. Nobody—least of all Edie, the daughter of the original owner—took seriously the "Positively No Loitering" sign. A couple of the guys acknowledged him with a two-fingered salute; the girls just giggled as they sucked on their soda bottles.

Nat "King" Cole was singing "Mona Lisa" on the jukebox as David walked through the door of the luncheonette. The scene never changed. The usual mental cases were hunched around the pin-ball machines, creating the usual racket as their well-practiced shots hit the gates and set the bells to ringing.

Most of the faces were familiar, and a strict hierarchy prevailed. The freshmen and sopho-mores were relegated to stools at the counter. The more exalted juniors and seniors were comfortably sprawled in their regular booths. Once graduated from high school, Edie's patrons were expected to move on and buy their nourishment at some other establishment. Edie had never been known to turn away a customer, but she didn't encourage any of the old-timers to stick around once they had earned their diplomas.

As long as they paid for their food and didn't swear, Edie didn't mind if a bunch of high school kids hung out in front of the shop. So what if they smoked cigarettes, tried to look tough, and flirted with each other? Edie figured she was doing their parents a favor, offering their children a place where she could keep an eye on them and make sure they stayed out of trouble.

She had a particularly soft spot in her heart for David, perhaps because she saw in his dark green eyes the vulnerability that came of having lost a parent too young. He was a good boy. He never sassed or gave her trouble, and he had a brain in his head. Not like some of those other punks who talked as if they, and not their parents, had just gotten off the boat.

Coming up on her forty-third birthday without a steady man in her bed, Edie had given up hoping she would ever have her own kids. But David Greene was just the kind of boy she would have wanted. She couldn't have been more thrilled for him than if he'd been her own son. Who ever heard of getting a football scholarship to a fancy boarding school? She was tickled to death that he had stopped by today so she could give him a proper send-off.

To David's acute embarrassment, she threw her arms around him and hugged him to her generous bosom.

"Hey, Edie," shouted Nick, "he's not goin' off to war, only Massachusetts!"

The rest of David's gang—Bear, Don, Mary Ellen, and Joyce—chortled at his wit.

Edie ignored the lot of them. She tore a bag of potato chips off the display rack and pressed it into David's hand. "Here, Davy," she said. "For the trip."

Don pretended to swoon with amazement. Edie was notorious for her strict no-credit, no-freebies policy.

Recovering, he cupped his palms to his mouth and declared, "Edie gives something away! Call Walter Winchell! I'm gonna have a heart attack."

"Frame it, Davy," yelled Nick.

"You go up there, Davy, and become a gentleman. Not like this riffraff," Edie said goodnaturedly, planting a big, wet kiss on his cheek.

David nodded a sheepish thank you. He was blushing bright red as he moved out of her embrace and went to join his friends in their booth.

Edie meant well, but the special attention embarrassed him. He hated being the one whom the teachers and other adults always turned to because he was smarter, more dependable, more likely to give them the answers they wanted. He hated feeling different. All he wanted was to be treated the same as all the other kids. Of course, it was precisely because he *was* different that St. Matthew's had come after him.

Bear wasn't about to let him forget it, either. "We oughtta be kickin' his skinny butt for breaking up the team," he said, grinning at David's discomfort.

"Yeah?" David playfully punched Bear's shoulder and claimed his share of the bench. "Who's holding you back?"

That was all the invitation his pals needed. Nick and Don grabbed his arms while Bear locked his head in a hammer hold.

"Hey!" Edie protested. "Hey! You wanna stay in here?" Her hands planted firmly on her hips, she stood glaring at the lot of them. No fighting was allowed in her place, not even in jest.

The boys released David from their grip and sat back, smiling up at her like three innocent little choirboys. She frowned a final warning and moved on to the next table to add up the bill.

Joyce and Mary Ellen rolled their eyes at her retreating back and struggled to contain their giggles. Joyce was madly in love with David. She had adored him unreservedly and unrequitedly since tenth grade, when she had sat behind him in Mrs. Murphy's English class. They had gone to lots of parties together, but always in a group. He had never even tried to kiss her. Joyce couldn't bear to think about how much she would miss him.

"If I had your brains, I'd go, too," said Bear.

Mary Ellen looked pained. She and Bear had gone steady since last Christmas, and she hated for him to talk about anything that didn't involve her. But Bear wasn't really interested in leaving Scranton. He couldn't even spell Massachusetts, he had joked, much less think about going to school there.

"His brains? *Any* brains," joked Nick, who had almost been dropped from the team for flunking three of his five courses.

Bear grabbed a handful of french fries off his plate. "Yeah?" he taunted him. "Look who's talkin'."

"I don't know," said David, speaking as much to himself as to his friends.

"What?" said Bear.

David shrugged. Seated here among his friends, anticipating how he would feel tomorrow when he would wake up in a strange room, he was having serious second thoughts. "I don't know about that place."

"You know it's not *this* place," Bear cracked. He reached for the bottle of ketchup, but his hand froze in midmotion as the unmistakable sound of motorcycle engines suddenly filled the air. He leaned out of the booth and squinted through the smudged glass window.

"Aw, shit. Kocus," he mumbled, spotting the four Harleys that had pulled up in front of Edie's.

David turned around and saw that Steve Kocus was hunched over his bike, smoking a cigarette and laughing with his biker pals. "So what?"

Kocus's gang liked to dress and talk tough. But an uneasy truce had been struck between the bikers and the football team. Each group generally steered clear of the other. When one of them did venture onto the other's territory, as the bikers had by showing up at Edie's, the action was usually limited to insults and threats.

Bear grinned and pulled David aside so the girls couldn't hear what he was about to say. "Night before last," he told David, "his sister gave me a hand job. It was her idea."

As if that made a difference. The guy's sister could have sent Bear a written invitation, and Kocus would still feel the need to defend his sister's honor. She was dumb enough to tell him, and he was dumb enough to beat her up, then come after Bear. Kocus had just about killed the last jerk who had laid a hand on his sister.

But Bear was the dumbest one of them all. He had bragged to David that Mary Ellen put out for him whenever he wanted, so wasn't that enough? Besides, David thought, even if he were lying about Mary Ellen, why did he have to go looking for trouble? Kocus's sister wasn't even all that cute.

The girls exchanged nervous looks, and Mary Ellen tried to grab Bear's arm, but he brushed her aside. Hurt by his rejection, she sat back and shrugged, as if to say, I don't care. Go ahead. Get yourself killed. But the expression on her face betrayed her fear.

A tense silence fell over the luncheonette as David and the rest of the guys followed Bear outside. The door slammed shut behind them. Kocus and his buddies sat at the curb, straddling their bikes, a vengeful posse come to even the score and restore his sister's honor.

Numberwise, the two groups were evenly matched, four against four. The football players outweighed the bikers by a good seventy-five pounds and were in much better physical condition. But the bikers were known to carry knives and chains that would appear in a flash if they were losing a fistfight.

David felt as if he were watching a play in which he was both participant and onlooker. Part of him was mad as hell at Bear for having gotten himself into such a mess. It was too nice a day to be rumbling with Kocus. But another part of him felt a surge of excitement as the two groups faced off. Whatever doubts he had about St. Matthew's had been replaced by the certainty that he was ready to jump right in if Bear needed him.

Kocus threw his cigarette onto the pavement, ground it out with his heel, and glared at David. Then he said, "Hey, Bear."

"Hey, Kocus." Bear nodded.

"We was thinkin' about goin' in there." Kocus smirked. "You know, eat somethin'?"

The three other bikers guffawed. David didn't get the joke, but he figured he wasn't missing much. Kocus wasn't about to get himself elected class clown.

Bear took a step closer, as if to remind the bikers that they were encroaching on his turf, and shook his head. "I don't think it would be a good idea."

"Why not?" Kocus stared long and hard at

13

David, loudly cleared his throat, and let fly a thick gob of spit. Then he said, "They let Jews in there."

Kocus's pals thought he was a regular comedian. One of them was laughing so hard that he almost fell off his bike.

Kocus leered at David, all but begging for a swift, hard punch in his fat mouth. Was the biker zeroing in on him because he figured David to be a less threatening rival than Bear?

David clenched his fists behind his back and tried to control his anger. He could sense Bear shifting his weight, readying himself for the brawl. Okay, they would fight if they had to. But first Kocus deserved to get a taste of his own nasty medicine.

"Your sister can come in," said David in a calm, even tone. "Only she'll have to wash her hands."

Now it was his friends' turn to chuckle. Bear's shoulders shook with mirth. David smiled at Kocus, daring him to return the volley.

The biker's face had turned a bright purple. It occurred to David that Kocus wasn't about to broadcast to the world that his sister had given Bear a hand job. His friends probably didn't know the reason for his beef with Bear.

Kocus narrowed his eyes. "You got a Jew friend with a smart mouth," he said to Bear.

Bear glanced at David and shrugged. "Yeah," he said agreeably. "I guess I do."

"So it don't bother you they killed Jesus 'n' everything?"

They. David took a deep breath and tried to control his temper.

This wasn't the first time some stupid jerk-off had come after him just because he was Jewish. The nasty comments had started as far back as grammar school. David had come home crying because one of the kids had accused him of killing some guy named Jesus. His mother had pulled him up onto her lap and kissed his tears away and tried to explain to him about anti–Semitism.

He could still remember his puzzlement. Who was Auntie Semitism? How did his classmates know this awful aunt of his, when he'd never heard of her before? And why were they blaming him for whatever it was *she* had done?

For a long time he had secretly hated his newly discovered relative. He had lived with the fear that she might someday show up in Scranton and destroy whatever chance he had of being accepted by the other kids. As it was, they thought it strange that he went to church on Saturday instead of Sunday; that he called his church a synagogue, a word that most of them couldn't even pronounce; that he sometimes stayed home from school because his holidays were different from theirs.

Luckily, he could run faster and jump farther than just about anyone else in first grade. When their teacher taught them how to play red rover and kickball, everyone wanted to be on his team. By the end of the year he had so many friends that he had stopped wishing his parents would celebrate Christmas so he could be just the same as everybody else.

The older he got, the less it hurt when some asshole made fun of him for being Jewish. His grandpa had explained to him that people who felt bad about their lives often needed a scapegoat, someone to whom they could point as the cause of their problems. In Poland, where Grandpa had lived until he was twenty-three, the Jews had always been the target of prejudice and anger. Unfortunately, some of their neighbors here in Scranton believed in handing that tradition down to their children. They needed to learn that such old-country ways had no place in America.

David had followed Grandpa's advice and bloodied more than a few noses before his father found out how he was dealing with the name-callers. Fighting was for uneducated peasants, Alan Greene had declared. He wasn't raising his son to be a street brawler. If David needed to hit something, his father would buy him a punching bag. Otherwise, he was to save his tackling for the football field.

Except for an occasional battle with the odd jerk who could be silenced only with a show of physical force, David had respected Pop's wishes. At school his religion simply wasn't an issue. It didn't seem to matter to Bear or any of the other guys on the team whether David was Jewish, Catholic, or Moslem.

So what if he ate matzo at Passover instead of chocolate Easter eggs and jelly beans? If he had to fast once a year on Yom Kippur instead of giving up ice cream for Lent? If he lit a Hanukkah menorah for eight days in December instead of putting up a Christmas tree?

Big deal. Without David there to call the plays, Scranton never would have won the league championship. Nor was Bear as likely to have led the league in rushing. Not that their friendship was only about football. They were buddies. They hung together after school, double-dated, lent each other money when one of them ran a few bucks short between allowances.

Whoever *they* were who had killed Jesus had nothing to do with David Greene.

Bear stretched his hands and cracked his knuckles, one by one. "Naw," he said. "It don't bother me. Didn't know the man."

"Yeah, I guess it was a long time ago," Kocus conceded. He cleared his throat and spat again. The gob of saliva landed only inches away from David's boot. "But it still bothers the shit outta me, you sheenie bastard."

David's heart was pounding very hard and fast. He was aware of nothing but the slobber seeping into the dry ground at his feet and the smug, thinly disguised hatred on Kocus's face. Whatever had happened between Bear and the biker's sister was beside the point. Kocus was spoiling for a battle. He had gone out of his way to make it a personal matter between himself and David.

Sometimes the only way to educate the ignorant is with your hands, Grandpa had warned David. This was one of those times when his grandfather's philosophy made a whole lot more sense than his father's.

"Get off the bike," he told Kocus.

Kocus scowled menacingly at David. He swung his jeans-clad legs over the side of the Harley, snapped his fingers, and beckoned to his friends.

Then he swaggered toward the cramped, sunless alley that lay between the luncheonette and the next building.

The passageway, which opened onto the back alley at the other end, smelled of mold and dank and urine. It was strewn with broken bottles, ancient yellowed newspapers, and rotting garbage that seemed to have drawn every fly in the neighborhood. No more than four feet wide and hemmed in on either side, the passageway was an odd place for a fistfight. Nevertheless, hundreds of skirmishes had taken place there between teenagers like David and Kocus, seeking to teach a lesson or even a score.

Word of the match had spread among Edie's customers. They spilled out of the restaurant and gathered in knots at either end of the passageway to cheer and applaud as David and Kocus squared off against each other.

Kocus made the first move, throwing a swift, sure jab that caught David by surprise. He reeled backwards, smashed against the wall, and momentarily lost his balance. But he had kept himself in shape all summer with long runs and lots of sit-ups. Now his training paid off as he made a quick recovery and sprang at Kocus with all the grace of Sugar Ray Robinson dancing around Carl "Bobo" Olson.

He struck hard with both hands. His right fist connected with Kocus's nose, his left with Kocus's shoulder. Kocus hooked his arm around David's neck and returned the blow. The onlookers screamed their support as first one, then the other seized the advantage.

David was oblivious to their cries. He was conscious only of his overwhelming need to punish his opponent. Kocus was a bully who got his kicks by roaring around town on his Harley, trying to frighten anyone who had neither brains nor guts enough to see through his scare tactics. Pop believed that bullies were to be pitied, not hated. But at this moment Kocus's face, pressed up so close to his, had become the face of every person who had ever teased or slurred David for being Jewish. A blinding, venomous rage fueled the power of his punches.

Tightly confined within the narrow gap that separated the brick-walled buildings, the boys pummeled each other with their hands and elbows and knees. There was so little room to maneuver in the darkness that at times they seemed to be locked together in a clumsy embrace that was broken only by their feints and swings.

Kocus was bigger, but David was the better athlete. He could almost feel his grandfather there by his side, rooting for him to win, as he forced Kocus to his knees. A sharp poke brought Kocus down to the ground. David straddled him and unloaded a barrage of hard, vicious hits that had the biker groaning in protest.

Bear could call a TKO when he saw one. "That's enough," he said, pulling David away from Kocus before he killed the guy.

"I ain't beat," Kocus grunted with more bravado than honesty.

"The hell you ain't. Get him on his bike," Bear ordered Kocus's henchmen.

Kocus's nose and lip were already starting to swell, and he was spitting blood. But he shrugged off his pals and glowered at David. "I ain't beat," he mumbled. Then, stumbling like a boxer who'd endured a few too many rounds, he shouldered his way through the crowd and limped back to his bike.

The excitement over, the spectators returned to Edie's to order another round of sodas and analyze the match. David slid down to the ground to recover.

Gingerly rubbing his sore jaw, he grinned at Bear and said, "I thought this was supposed to be *your* fight."

"That's okay. You can handle my small stuff," Bear joked.

Don stared through the gloom at the bruises on David's face. "Jesus, Davy," he mumbled. "You don't look so good."

He didn't feel so good either. Kocus was a mean son of a gun, and the win hadn't come easily. He touched his fingertips to his forehead and winced at the lump that was beginning to form there.

"God!" He shook his head and pulled himself up to his feet. "I gotta clean up. My old man . . ."

There was no need to finish the sentence. The other guys knew just what he was thinking. How was he ever going to explain all the scrapes and swelling to his father?

2

Though only a mild breeze was blowing from the west, a thick cloud of coal dust swirled about the heads of the two men who stood talking on the elevated walkway. Several hundred feet below them enormous lumps of coal came tumbling like oversized dice through a chute into the coal breaker, there to be crushed into more easily transportable chunks. The noise created by the process was deafening. But both men had put in so many thousands of hours within earshot of the breaker that they automatically pitched their voices above the din as they carried on their conversation.

The foreman and younger of the two, Alan Greene, was keeping one eye out for his son as he issued some last-minute instructions to Del Hawkins, the point man on his crew. David's father was that rare exception among the supervisory staff at the mine: He was both liked and respected by his workers.

He had put in his first shift at the mine the summer before he graduated from high school; he had never intended to make it his life's work. But the money was decent and the work was steady, so he'd postponed going to college. And then he had met David's mother. . . .

Alan sighed. If only Dorothy were alive today to see her beloved firstborn son going off to study at one of the finest prep schools in the country. A school that normally accepted only the smartest boys from America's richest and most important families. Not that David wasn't every bit as bright and talented as any of the other students. But how often did a Jewish kid—the son of a mine worker —get handed such a scholarship? That David should have been invited to attend St. Matthew's was practically a miracle.

Del was smiling now and pointing. Finally, here was David, driving Alan's car into the yard past the massive open coal pit. Alan glanced at his watch. The boy was late. If they didn't hurry, he might miss the bus.

He wished he could take David to school himself. He wasn't happy about his son having to ride the bus all the way to Massachusetts alone. But despite his seniority, it didn't seem wise, in these economically troubled times, to turn down an overtime shift or ask for extra time off.

In the end, it didn't much matter whether David went by bus, car, or private plane so long as he got to St. Matthew's in one piece. Thank God, the boy was responsible enough to travel on his own. Alan supposed there weren't a lot of fathers who could say the same for their kids.

He walked quickly down the steps and strode past the huge, sprawling mine machinery that was so much a part of his daily vista he hardly even noticed it. A couple of the old-timers, knowing this was a red-letter day for the Greene family, smiled at Alan and waved their good wishes.

The older Greene had a reputation for being fair and trustworthy, for keeping his promises, for being willing to give the fellows a break. Their affection for him extended to his son, whom most of them had known from the time he was just learning to walk, when he would toddle around after his dad with obvious, wide-eyed admiration. Now the boy was a football champ, famous enough that people had heard of him all the way east in Massachusetts.

"Give 'em hell, kid!" hollered Weezer, the scale attendant, as David pulled up at the weigh station.

David flashed a grin of thanks at Weezer, who looked like an ancient, shrunken elf seated on his perch next to the scale. David always got a kick out of Weezer. The guy had some terrific stories to tell about the old days. He had been around so long he had actually marched shoulder to shoulder with the great union leader, John L. Lewis.

Today, however, there was no time for stories.

"You're late." Alan Greene stated the obvious as he slid into the passenger's seat.

Any number of answers came to mind, but David kept his mouth shut. He *knew* he was late. So why did Pop have to remind him?

Determined to preserve the peace, David averted his head and tried to hide his battered face from his father.

The worst of the damage had been done to the left side, and the area above his left eye was throbbing. But Kocus had managed to leave his mark on David's right cheek as well.

"Stop the car," said his father, who would have had to be blind not to notice the rapidly purpling bruise.

David grimaced. Here came trouble. He turned off the ignition and steeled himself for Pop's explosion.

"Look at me," his father demanded.

David reluctantly obeyed and turned to face him.

Pop's reaction was predictable. "Goddammit, David."

"I had to," David defended himself.

His father didn't believe in mincing words. "You get an opportunity like this, out of the blue, and you go off and pull this shit."

"I *had* to," David repeated.

Though he could see from Pop's expression that he wasn't buying the excuse, David was reluctant to offer any further explanation. They had gone over the same ground too often in the past. "Sticks and stones can break your bones, but words can never hurt you," his father always reminded him. Bullshit, David thought.

"This is a school that two presidents went to, a pipeline to Harvard University," his father said.

David stifled a yawn. He had heard this speech only about a million times since last February. Pop must have memorized the line from the St. Matthew's catalogue.

"They're gonna see you and think you're some kind of hoodlum." Alan Greene shook his head in disgust. "They might take one look at you and send you back."

The left side of David's head was beginning to ache. Pain made him reckless. "Fine," he said defiantly.

"Fine?" shouted his father. "Look around you, kid. You want this life?"

Pop knew just how to get to him. The answer to that one was simple: No. He didn't want Pop's life, or Weezer's, or the life of any of the other guys who could hope for nothing more than their union pension and a handshake from the boss when they retired.

But dammit, he'd had a reason, and a good one, to take on Kocus. "He called me a sheenie bastard. What was I supposed to do, walk away?"

"That's right, you walk away." His father nodded emphatically. He had walked away from a hell of a lot worse. "It ain't your problem. You can't fight your way through life like this."

"You never got into any fights?"

Because he didn't believe in lying to his son, he reluctantly admitted, "Yeah, I got into fights. But nobody ever handed me Harvard. Nobody ever handed me nothin'."

He paused to let the words sink in.

Or me either, thought David. I won that scholarship because I busted my butt in school and on the field. So how come I got to live my life for you?

"Your mother would have cried," his father said sorrowfully. "She would have sat down and cried."

David hated him for pulling out the big guilt gun. But of course, Pop was right. Mom used to get so upset by any kind of violence that she couldn't even watch him get tackled during a game. Now he really felt like a heel; his beaten-up face had reminded both of them how much they missed her.

He gritted his teeth. "I'm sorry," he said, eager to change the subject.

"You're sorry." His father shook his head. Then he folded his arms across his chest in resignation and said, "Let's go."

Sarah and Petey, the two youngest members of the Greene family, were already out in the yard, waiting impatiently for their father and brother to show up. Luckily for David, he had done all his packing the night before. Sarah had persuaded Petey to help her drag David's duffel bag out to the curb. All that was left was to load the bag into the trunk.

"You're going to miss the bus!" scolded Sarah, who had just turned fifteen and considered it her sacred duty to fuss over her father and brothers.

"Who'd you fight with?" asked Petey.

Their father shot David a warning glance. Twelve-year-old Petey looked up to his brother with respect bordering on hero worship. With the slightest encouragement Petey would follow David through a ring of fire. Alan didn't want his younger son taking up David's causes.

David winked at Petey, and then there was barely time enough for one last look at his home before Pop started the car. As they drove down the street David turned to stare at the brown row house with the yellow trim where he'd grown up. It looked much the same as the other houses on the block, except for the wide stripe of bare earth across the front lawn that commemorated David's earliest attempts to play football. He closed his eyes to fix the image in his memory: Petey's bike was leaning up against the steps, guarded by their next-door neighbor's cat, Pinky, who sat licking her fur and staring mournfully at David.

Though he and his parents had shared an apartment with Grandpa until just before Sarah was born, David couldn't remember living anywhere else but here. Suddenly he felt a twinge of dread at the thought of being so far away from everyone and everything that represented safety and familiarity.

The doubts he had felt earlier that morning echoed in his head. It dawned on him—and the realization came as a shock—that he was actually going to miss Sarah and Petey. He couldn't imagine how it would feel to wake up tomorrow morning without Petey curled in a ball in the other bed. Without Sarah yelling for him to hurry down before the toast got cold. Without Pop bugging him to read the whole newspaper, not just the sports section, because Harvard and Yale expected their students to keep up with current events.

Yeah . . . he would even miss Pop. As fathers went, Pop was okay. Sometimes, on a good day, he was actually terrific. But he could also be a real pain in the neck—much too strict and quick to criticize. Lately, without Mom around to calm him down, the slightest thing could make him lose his temper. Like today, for example. David could tell he was still angry. Sarah and Petey were fighting in the backseat, and Pop wasn't saying a word.

David wished he knew what Pop was thinking. Even more, he wished they could talk about what had happened without Pop getting so riled up and screaming about Harvard and Yale. He felt like there was something important Pop should be telling him now. Something that would help to banish the fingers of tension that were clutching at his stomach.

Was this how Pop had felt when he got drafted to fight in the Pacific? Naw . . . that made no sense. David was going to school, not war. Nobody would be pointing a gun at him. Besides, Pop always said that the army had made a man out of him. Maybe he figured that St. Matthew's would make a man out of David.

He imagined himself parading back and forth in front of his dormitory with a rifle slung over his shoulder and grinned. He ought to be happy it was a fancy prep school and not a goddamn military academy that had awarded him the scholarship!

They made it to the bus station with ten minutes to spare. While his father stood in line for his ticket David went to buy a candy bar and a Coke to wash down the chicken sandwiches Sarah had made for him to eat on the road. Then he rejoined his family outside. His brother and sister, as usual, were making pests of themselves, talking to the driver who was stowing his duffel bag in the baggage compartment. Luckily, the driver didn't seem to mind, probably because there were so few other passengers.

His father stood by the open bus door, smoking a cigarette and studying a map that showed the route the bus would follow. He hardly glanced up when David came over to join him. With the same grim look of annoyance on his face he handed David his ticket, along with the map. David knew that look only too well; it was hard for Pop to get over being mad, especially when one of his children had disappointed him.

"You can fit in if you really want to," he said, finally breaking the silence between them. "Or you can hack around with a chip on your shoulder."

David stared at the sign in the bus window: Scranton-Albany-Springfield-Boston. Pop was the one with the chip on his shoulder. What did he think? That David didn't want to make friends with the guys at St. Matthew's?

"Huh?" His father prompted him.

"All right, all right." David said, wishing his father would crack a smile. "I'll fit in."

"Listen, they came to you," his father reminded him. "You didn't come to them. You don't have to explain nothin' to nobody. Understand me?"

"All right," David quickly agreed, though he didn't understand at all what his father was trying to tell him. Of course the school had come to him. David had never even heard of St. Matthew's before they had sent their letter. Besides, what difference did it make? What was there to explain?

He nodded to mask his confusion. Finally his father smiled. "Say good-bye to your brother and sister," he said.

David leaned in to give Sarah a peck on the cheek. She surprised him by throwing her arms around him in a hug. The Greenes usually showed their affection with good-natured jabs and teasing words that were meant to convey how much they really did love one another.

As if surprised herself by her sudden show of affection, Sarah quickly pulled free and made a big fuss of smoothing down her bangs.

David put out his hand to shake Petey's, then jerked it away and tousled his hair instead. It was a tried-and-true routine, one that Petey fell for every time.

The driver walked past, boarded the bus, and settled himself in his seat. David gulped nervously. This was it.

"Change your shirt," his father said.

Apparently Pop was still too upset even to try and forgive what seemed to David like a rather minor crime. Hoping to spare himself another lecture on how to behave, David nodded and edged toward the bus.

But at the last minute his father surprised him. "What did the other guy look like?" he asked.

"Worse," said David, his face creasing in a grin of relief. He could feel the tension in his stomach disappearing as quickly as a quart of ice cream on a hot August afternoon.

His father took a step closer and impulsively placed his right palm on David's forehead. *"Mein lieber kind,"* he murmured, speaking in the Yiddish language he had learned from his father, *"gey gezinterheit."*

David didn't understand Yiddish. But he had heard those words often enough from his grandfather, who had communicated in a mishmash of Yiddish, English, and Polish, to know what they meant. My dear child, go in good health. Even after fifty years in America Grandpa had retained enough of his Polish–Jewish upbringing that he would thus bless any and all family members, even if they were going no further than the grocery store.

It was an open secret that David had been Grandpa Jack's favorite—the oldest son of his own firstborn son. Grandpa had died the year after David's bar mitzvah. Not long after that the varsity coach had begun scheduling extra football practices on Saturday mornings, and David had stopped going to synagogue except on the most important holidays. Now a long-buried memory, triggered by his father's pronouncing the familiar Yiddish phrase, suddenly resurfaced: the image of himself digging through Grandpa's jacket pocket for the two-cent miniature chocolate bars he always carried, to ease the boredom of the seemingly endless Sabbath morning services.

No other chocolate had ever tasted so good. But the same words that David had heard a million times from his grandfather felt unnatural, not to

31

mention embarrassing, when uttered by his father. "C'mon, Pop," he mumbled. "You're acting like Grandpa."

"You should be so lucky," scoffed his father, embarrassed himself at having been caught in such an uncharacteristic show of emotion. "Your grandfather revered education. If he had two dimes, one went for bread, one went for a book. I was a big disappointment to him. Married too young, started poppin' out kids."

Here came that same old tired song. David could have recited it in his sleep. So what was Pop's point? Did he regret having children? How the heck was that supposed to make David feel? Gee, sorry, Pop, for getting born. And if Pop didn't "revere education," as he'd put it, then who did? Because why else would David be getting on this bus, if not to go off and get the kind of education he couldn't get here in Scranton?

The joke was that Pop was becoming more and more like Grandpa every day, but David didn't want to be the one to break the news. "Gotta go, Dad," he said, extending his hand.

Again his father surprised him by planting a long, firm kiss on his cheek. "Go!" he said, choking back tears. He pushed David up the steps. "Make us proud."

3

Even the air smelled better in Massachusetts. It was cleaner and sweeter, like the flavor of fresh green peas newly picked from the garden. There was no rotten-egg odor of sulphur stinking up the town, no gray cloud of coal dust hovering in the atmosphere. In the grass behind the trim little building that doubled as train station and bus depot the crickets were shrilly proclaiming the end of summer. A trio of sparrows twittered overhead, welcoming David to the tiny town of Lebanon.

He might as well have been dropped on another planet. He took a deep breath, drank in the gentle taste of the late afternoon, and discovered pleasure. A couple of kids rode by on their bikes, laughing and eating Popsicles. Otherwise the street was as empty of traffic as the streets of Scranton had been earlier in the day. But the quiet felt different here: calmer and more peaceful, without the sense of gloomy resignation that always seemed to be skulking behind the boarded-up storefronts back home.

The lowering sun cast a long shadow on the spare white church that dominated the square across the road. Its slender steeple was topped by a large round clock. David squinted to read the time. Suddenly a bell began to count the hours. Five o'clock.

Mr. McDevitt, the football coach who had first spoken to David's father by phone, then come to visit them in Scranton, had promised to meet him in front of the depot at five. David hoped he hadn't forgotten. St. Matthew's was probably less than a mile up the hill that curved right at the end of the block. But his duffel bag was heavy, and he hated the idea of showing up at his dorm hot and sweaty from having carried the bag all the way there.

On the other hand, he felt silly, standing all by himself, jingling the change in his pockets because he had nothing better to do. The hike up the hill could be a good workout, he decided. Like doing a set of reps with the barbells.

He hoisted the duffel across his left shoulder just as Coach McDevitt appeared around the corner.

"Greene!" he called out, waving to get David's attention. "Over here."

Relieved to see him, David smiled and waved back. "Hi, Coach."

The coach seemed like a stand-up guy: tough but fair. In Scranton he had taken David and his father out for dinner and talked to them about St. Matthew's, where he'd been head of the coaching staff for the last seven years. He had made no secret of the fact that his background was a lot closer to Alan Greene's than to his students'.

He'd grown up in Lowell, a factory town up north near New Hampshire. He had learned a thing or two at St. Matthew's, he'd said. How to dress. How to hold a knife, and which fork to use for eating salad. How to talk to the men who got elected to the Senate, made millions of dollars on Wall Street, owned the companies that ran the coal mines and the clothing factory where his own mother had worked so he could go to college.

He had learned all kinds of little things that counted for a lot in the world. "You know what I mean?" he'd asked Alan Greene, taking a long swallow of scotch.

Though Mr. McDevitt was only eleven years older than Pop, David's father had gazed at him almost worshipfully and nodded his understanding. Yes, he certainly did know what Mr. McDevitt meant. He hoped, he told the coach, that David would also come to understand how important it was to learn those same lessons.

The coach was eyeing the bruises on David's face.

"I had a little accident," David explained.

"You all right?"

David shrugged. It probably looked much worse than it felt. "Yeah, it's nothing."

"Here," said the coach, grabbing David's duffel. "Lemme get that for you."

His car was parked behind the general store next to the depot. "How was the trip?" he asked, heading up the hill.

"Fine," David said, feeling nervous again the closer he got to the school.

"Your father?"

David ran his tongue around the inside of his mouth, which felt as if it were stuffed with cotton. "He's fine."

"He excited?" the coach wanted to know.

Understatement of the year, thought David. But somehow it seemed as if he would be betraying his dad to admit that. So all he said was "Yeah."

"You're gonna love these kids," the coach assured him, as if sensing his trepidation. "They're a great bunch."

David stared out the car window, waiting to get his first glimpse of St. Matthew's. He had studied the pictures in the catalogue, but he'd never stopped to wonder what the town itself looked like. He guessed that the people who lived here were richer than most of the folks he knew in Scranton. The houses, which were set back from the road and partly hidden from view by tall, leafy trees, looked more like hotels than private homes.

"They're all looking forward to meeting you," the coach said, turning right through the curlicued wrought-iron gates that guarded the main entrance to the school grounds.

Two elaborately carved stone urns, which reminded David of those he'd seen in a book on ancient Greek art, rested atop the massive brick pillars that stood on either side of the gates. Even more impressive was the sign that rested above the gates like some sort of crown or medieval crest of honor, emblazoned with the words "St. Matthew's Academy for Boys."

As Coach McDevitt slowly crossed the campus David surveyed the rolling lawns and ivy-covered buildings. A bell—the same one David had heard earlier—marked the quarter hour from the tower that rose above the administration building. The clear, delicate chimes drifted through the pink-tinged predusk sky, signaling the parents who were helping their sons get settled that the boys were shortly due in chapel.

Outside of the Cadillac dealership showroom in Scranton's ritziest section, David had never seen so many Caddys parked in one place, nor so many sleekly built woody wagons. He even counted a handful or two of long, black limousines, driven by chauffeurs dressed in sharp, military-style uniforms.

David gawked at the families gathered in knots in front of the various buildings. They all had the same look about them. The men were tall and handsome, the women beautiful enough to have walked out of a magazine advertisement. They seemed so happy and self-confident, so blond and well-fed and rich.

Two little boys dressed in matching blue blazers, striped shirts, and khaki shorts ran by the coach's car and flashed identical smiles at David through the window. Right behind them came a tall, thin boy carrying a pair of covered tennis rackets in one hand, a massive dictionary in the other. Their older brother, David guessed.

"Jesus!" He whistled. *"This* is a high school?"

The coach grinned at David's reaction. "Yeah, it's *your* high school."

Another student, wearing chinos and a blue oxford shirt, was lugging a well-padded armchair up the steps of one of the dorms. The sign on the front said "Iselin Hall," which was the name of the dorm to which David had been assigned. The boy flicked his blond hair out of his eyes and stopped to chat with a couple of the other students who were likewise bringing luggage and pieces of furniture into the building.

David couldn't make out what they were saying, but he could hear their loud, easy laughter. He watched for a moment as one boy, a redhead whose easy grin reminded him of Bear, clowned for the rest of the crew. From the looks of it, they all seemed to have known one another for years.

He pulled his duffel bag out of the backseat and hoisted it up to his shoulder. Trying not to sound as daunted as he felt at the prospect of making friends with the other students, he said, "Thanks for the lift, Coach. See you at practice."

"Wait a minute." McDevitt crooked a finger, summoned him over to the car window, and spoke almost in a whisper. "I meant to ask you . . . you got any diet problems?"

David stared at him blankly. "Diet problems?"

"Any stuff you can't eat?"

A light bulb went off in David's head. He almost laughed aloud when he realized what the coach was referring to. In his roundabout way, Coach

McDevitt wanted to know whether David kept the laws of kashruth, which forbade eating shellfish as well as ham, bacon, or any other pork products.

David figured that it was nobody's business what he did or didn't eat. He pretended to ponder the question. Finally he said, "I can't eat turnips."

"Turnips," the coach said, considering David's response. "Can't eat 'em myself." Then he smiled and lowered his voice even more. "Listen, everybody's gonna be a little curious about you."

"I'm a little curious about them," said David.

"I mean"—the coach cleared his throat—"nobody ever comes here for just the last year. It's an unusual situation."

Still unclear about where the conversation was going, David kept silent.

"Don't get me wrong," the coach said. "They're a great bunch of kids, but . . . they're privileged. They take things for granted you and me never would."

What things? David wondered. So what if their families were richer than his? Pop gave him whatever he needed—sports equipment, clothes, money for the movies. He'd never had to go to bed hungry or been forced to walk to school, the way his father had during the Depression.

"Just play your cards close to the vest, that's my advice," Coach McDevitt said.

David wished the coach would stop sounding so mysterious. "What do you mean?"

The coach shrugged. "It's an expression. It means you shouldn't tell people any more than they

39

need to know." Suddenly his voice got louder, his tone more cheerful. He clapped David on the shoulder and said, "Hey, see you in practice."

He hit the gas and was gone before David had a chance to say good-bye.

The corridors of Iselin Hall were well-trafficked with boys bumping into one another and banging against the walls as they struggled to get their trunks and suitcases up the stairs. Many of them glanced inquiringly at David as he passed by, lugging his duffel bag down the hallway in search of his room. He rechecked the letter that Pop had received from the headmaster listing his room assignment as well as his roommate.

"St. Matthew's prides itself," said the letter, "on its comfortable accommodations, which are designed to accustom our young men to the niceties of gracious adult living. Iselin Hall, named for one of our most illustrious graduates, houses a dormitory master who resides on the first floor and is responsible for the sixteen students in each of the four entryways. David will be sharing a two-room suite (living room and bedroom) with Christopher Reece, an honor student who is well suited to the task of familiarizing your son with the regulations and traditions that make St. Matthew's the very special place it is."

Niceties of gracious adult living? David thought. A dormitory master? Regulations and traditions?

Impressed though he was with anything that had to do with St. Matthew's, even Pop had laughed at the headmaster's fancy phrases and high-toned language. Now it was David's turn to be impressed as he gaped through the open doorways at the cozily furnished suites, many of which appeared to have been recently redecorated by somebody's mom.

Did these rooms really belong to students? Some of them were nicer than his own living room at home!

A handsome, athletic-looking boy maneuvered past David with a large suitcase perched flat on his head. Balanced on top of the suitcase was a pair of black leather ice skates with gleaming, razor-sharp blades. The guy probably played ice hockey, David decided. Coach had mentioned that St. Matthew's had a championship hockey team.

His room was almost at the end of the corridor. As he dropped his bag in the middle of the living room four boys rushed out of the room across the hall to greet him.

One of them stuck out his hand and said, "Hi, you finally got here."

"Yeah," said David, wishing his jacket were any other color than maroon.

"I'm Chris Reece," the first boy said. "Your roommate."

Christopher Reece, he thought. The honor student. "Oh, hi. David Greene."

Chris pointed to each boy in turn as he introduced them. "This is Charlie Dillon, Jack Connors, Rip Van Kelt."

David's first impression was that except for Jack, who had wavy red hair and fair skin, the boys

41

exemplified what the girls back home would have called "tall, dark, and handsome." They were all similarly dressed, in button-down white shirts, perfectly creased chinos, and black or brown penny loafers.

All of a sudden David felt grubby from the bus ride. He looked down at his own unpolished loafers and noticed a grease stain just above the crotch of his pants. Brushing away a sprinkling of potato-chip crumbs, he nodded at his impromptu welcoming committee.

"We're the big men on campus," Charlie Dillon said, vigorously shaking David's hand.

Sure that Charlie was joking, David laughed.

"It's true," an absolutely straight-faced Dillon assured him.

Connors was gobbling peanuts, tossing them up in the air and catching them with his tongue. "Where you from, Greene?" he wanted to know.

"Scranton, P-A," David said.

"Scranton?" The way Connors pronounced it, David might as well have admitted to coming from another planet.

Reece glanced sideways at David, as if to apologize for his friend's rudeness. "That's like in America, Connors," he said.

"No shit?"

"You know," said Dillon, his dark blue eyes gleaming wickedly, "you're the very first ringer St. Matthew's has ever hired."

"C'mon, Dillon." Reece shook his head. "Lay off."

"He is. That's something of an honor," Dillon insisted. But his mocking attitude belied his words. "Aren't you honored, Greene?"

David wondered why the guy was giving him such a hard time. They had only just met, but Dillon already seemed to be harboring a grudge against him. "I haven't thought about it," he said truthfully.

"You must be about the best high school quarterback money can buy." Dillon continued to needle him.

Connors made a face. "Hey, Dillon," he admonished his friend. Then he turned to David and said, "Don't pay any attention. You want some peanuts?"

David poured himself a handful and tipped them into his mouth. "No problem," he said. "Even in Scranton a prick is a prick."

There was a moment of silence as the boys digested David's comeback. Had he gone too far and screwed himself by making fun of one of the big men on campus? he wondered. The year ahead could quickly become a living nightmare if these guys turned against him on his first day.

On the other hand, he had to show them that David Greene from Scranton, Pa., wasn't a ninety-pound hick weakling to be mocked and pushed around.

Yes, their clothes were nicer, and they talked faster and smoother than he did. But his presence here at St. Matthew's hadn't been sought after because his family had lots of money, or because his father and grandfather were alumni. The school wanted him—*needed* him—to help its football team win games. Just wait till they saw what he could do on the field. And until then, just let them *try* to make a monkey out of him!

Dillon turned out to be a better sport than David would have guessed. "You don't have to be so sensitive," he said with a smile. "It's not required here."

He put out his hand in a gesture of conciliation. "There was some talk about me playing quarterback this year," he reluctantly admitted, seeming to sense David's hesitation. "So you know . . ."

No wonder the guy was coming on like such a jerk. David shook Dillon's hand and returned the smile. He understood how these things happened. It never felt good to be the odd man out, the one who got bumped because someone else was bigger, stronger, or smarter.

"I'm sorry," broke in Rip Van Kelt, the same thin boy David had noticed earlier carrying tennis rackets and a dictionary. He was the tallest of the group, and from his expression, the most serious. "I gotta ask. Were you in an accident or something?"

He had been staring at David throughout his exchange with Dillon. Now David realized why. His bruised cheek and swollen eye.

"I had a little fight," David said curtly.

Undeterred by his brusqueness, Van Kelt pressed on. "A fight?" His brown eyes widened with curiosity. "A fistfight?"

"Yeah," David replied, choosing his words carefully. He didn't want to earn himself a reputation as a troublemaker. But if these guys were going to be impressed because he and Kocus had gone at it in the alleyway and messed up each other's faces, what the heck? "A kind of . . . going-away fight."

"Like a rumble?" demanded Connors, dropping a peanut in his excitement.

For a moment David thought he was being ribbed again. Did Connors really believe that he and his pals were juvenile delinquents who lived in a slum, like the New York City hoods in *The Blackboard Jungle,* which had played at the movies last spring?

But Dillon wasn't joking. In fact, it slowly dawned on David that the boys were almost *begging* him to confirm that he was a tough kid from a bad neighborhood who had to defend his right to cross the street.

"Yeah," he allowed. He crossed his fingers behind his back. "Kind of like a rumble."

Connors whistled long and loudly. "Wow! A rumble."

"Over girls and stuff?" Van Kelt wanted to know.

"There's this place we hang out at, and these guys wanted to come in. Motorcycle guys. We wouldn't let them," David said, taking some poetic license.

"Wow," Connors repeated.

Van Kelt needed clarification. "You didn't want them on your turf, right?"

"Right." David nodded.

"That's understandable," Connors said approvingly. "Everybody knows you can't just go on somebody else's turf."

David nodded again and wished they would drop the subject before he told any outright lies. He was about to take matters into his own hands by asking about the football team when a high-pitched voice suddenly echoed in the hallway outside their room.

"'Who knows what evil lurks in the hearts of men? The Shadow knows,'" the voice declared, imitating the exaggerated accent and intonation of the actor who announced the weekly radio show that all the boys listened to.

The owner of the voice appeared in the doorway, dressed as the Shadow in a dark hat, sunglasses, and a long, dark raincoat.

"McGivern! My roomie!" shouted Connors happily.

"'The weed of crime bears bitter fruit. Crime does not pay. The Shadow knows.'" Punctuating his remarks with an eerie cackle, McGivern peered around the room as if in search of anyone audacious enough to have committed a crime without paying the penalty.

While Connors and Dillon tussled affectionately with him, David stared at McGivern. Beneath his peculiar attire he looked like a fairly normal fellow, somewhat shorter than the others, with a sunburned nose and an impish grin.

"C'mon, meet my roommate," said Reece, acting as if McGivern's behavior were nothing out of the ordinary. "David Greene. The new quarterback."

McGivern stepped forward and shook David's

hand. Then, without any warning, he threw his arms around David's shoulders in a warm embrace.

The other boys seemed amused, but David was stunned. This was *too* weird. Whoever heard of a guy hugging another guy?

"Football is a game for cretins, bug squashers, and criminals. Don't you agree?" asked McGivern, squinting at David above his half-lowered sunglasses.

Connors snorted with laughter as Dillon explained, "Mac wants to play, but he's too frail."

"This is true," Van Kelt agreed in his earnest, slow-speaking way. "So we let him be student manager."

The boys guffawed loudly. McGivern whirled around and dug a sharp elbow in the general vicinity of Van Kelt's gut. Then he hissed like an angry cat who'd been shocked out of a deep sleep and sprang out of the room. His eerie giggle trailed behind him as he disappeared from sight.

David glanced inquiringly at Reece, who only smiled and shrugged in response. Then Connors, Dillon, and Van Kelt decided they had better get moving as well. It was almost six o'clock, and not one of them dared to be less than punctual for First Chapel. After all, they had to set an example for the rest of the students.

A few minutes later, unpacking his bag in the bedroom of the suite, David considered one fundamental difference between St. Matthew's and Scranton High. Back home a guy like McGivern would have been shunned by everyone but the weirdos. Yet here, in spite of (or perhaps because of) his eccentricities, he appeared to be not only accepted but well-liked.

David supposed that was a good sign. Maybe the boys would accept him, too, instead of rejecting him as an outsider who dressed and talked differently.

The bedroom had two beds at one end, two narrow closets and twin mirrored dressers at the other. Reece had already filled up one closet and claimed his bed, so David threw a pair of sheets and a blanket on top of the other. He would make the bed up after supper. In the meantime he pulled out a clean pair of pants and hung up the navy blue blazer with the school insignia on the left lapel pocket that was part of the required dress uniform.

Reece was lying on his bed, watching David get dressed. "I guess you didn't get a school tie yet," he said, noticing the one that David had chosen.

David shook his head. Following the instructions they had received in one of the many letters from St. Matthew's, his father had sent in an order for two of the specially tailored school blazers. Either Pop had forgotten to order the ties, or for some reason he'd decided they weren't necessary. David hadn't paid much attention to the subject himself. Sarah had been far more intrigued than he by the idea of a uniform.

Reece got up, went over to his well-stocked closet, and pulled off a hanger one of several neatly folded red and blue striped ties. "You can wear this one," he said, offering it to David. "I have extras because I'm always dragging them through the soup."

"Thanks." Grateful for his roommate's tact, David fitted the tie around his collar, straightened the knot, and slipped on his corduroy jacket.

"You mind if I ask?" Reece said. "How'd you wind up here?"

David hesitated, recalling Coach's earlier words of advice. "I'm not supposed to talk about it."

"Let me guess," Reece said, examining his face in the mirror. "Coach McDevitt paid you a visit, said you could qualify for an alumni scholarship."

David glanced at his roommate. He was exactly on target. "Good guess. How'd you know?"

"St. Luke's has whipped us three years in a row. The alumni are pissed. They want a win real bad. Not too much pressure, huh?"

It was a lot of pressure, but that was just how David liked to play. The closer the game, the more focused he became on winning. He preferred to come in as the underdog, the long shot who surprised the crowd by stealing the win when his opponent least expected it. He was about to explain this to Reece when their suite door suddenly swung open. A pale, scrawnily built boy with neatly combed, perfectly straight blond hair poked his head into the room.

"This the guy?" he demanded.

Reece nodded. "This is the guy. David Greene, meet Magoo."

The boy wore wire-rimmed glasses so thick that his blue eyes seemed magnified behind the lenses.

"Hi," said David, fighting to stifle his laughter as

he realized how much the boy reminded him of Mr. Magoo, the squat-faced, nearsighted cartoon character.

"My name happens to be Richard Collins," Magoo quickly corrected Reece.

"The blind Mr. Magoo," Reece said sotto voce.

"I've worn these specs since I was six," Magoo explained, managing to sound simultaneously miserable and resigned about the situation.

"Hey, this the guy?" Yet another face appeared in the doorway. He was much huskier than Magoo, with a football player's broad shoulders and chest.

His square jaw was thrust forward and his deep-set, narrow brown eyes carefully appraised David as he put out his hand.

"Chesty Smith, David Greene," Reece said.

"Hi," David said, shaking Chesty's hand.

"This summer I got into a fight," Chesty informed him.

"Yeah?" So word must have gotten around about his "rumble," because Chesty seemed eager to impress him with this announcement. David figured that Kocus had done him a favor by picking that fight.

"Yeah. He was twenty years old. Went to Cornell. I beat the shit out of him," Chesty boasted.

"Good," David said, not quite sure what Chesty expected from him.

Magoo, who had been circling David like a nearsighted bee buzzing about a patch of clover, suddenly reached over and took hold of David's lapel between his two fingers. Peering through his thick lenses, he carefully inspected the material.

"Take my advice," he said, making a face. "Incinerate the jacket."

"Here, try this one." Chesty handed his to David. "I got a million of 'em."

"Big man," hooted Magoo.

Chesty lunged, grabbed his sidekick in a headlock, and hustled him out of the room.

"I dress pretty awful, huh?" David said once he and Reece had stopped laughing at the pair's antics. He had never much cared about his wardrobe, but now the cut and color of his clothes suddenly seemed important.

"Don't worry." Reece gave him an encouraging clap on the back and led the way out of the room. "We'll put you together."

Dusk had almost fallen, and the chapel bell was tolling an insistent summons to the throng of students pouring out of the dorms. They jostled and yelled at one another as they tramped across the grassy quadrangle toward the spire-topped, plain white building that served as the focal point of the campus. David easily kept pace with Reece and his classmates, who already seemed to have accepted him as one of their gang. It didn't appear to matter that he still felt somewhat shy and inhibited in their midst. The seven boys included him in their breezy flow of jokes as naturally as if they had known and liked him for years.

"You gotta go to chapel three times a week," Reece told him.

David remembered reading in the school handbook about required chapel attendance, though at the time he hadn't stopped to wonder exactly what went on there.

"Nobody's figured out why," said Van Kelt.

"The only reason we go is to pray we beat St. Luke's," Dillon chortled.

McGivern, now stripped of his sunglasses and cape, added glumly, "You've seen one church, you've seen them all. Like western movies."

David didn't really understand the comparison between church interiors and Westerns. But he kept his mouth shut and tried to look as if he knew what McGivern was talking about.

"You're going straight to hell, Mac," Connors chided his roommate.

"They make you fill out an attendance slip," said Dillon, who seemed to have forgiven David for taking his place on the team.

With a sideways glance at Van Kelt, Magoo broke in. "But you can bribe somebody."

"Yeah." Chesty agreed. "They'll go for you."

"I didn't hear that," Van Kelt said quickly.

David glanced at him to see if he was kidding. Paying to get out of chapel wasn't exactly a crime. Why would Van Kelt be so offended by the idea that it couldn't even be discussed in his presence? Could the guy really be that straight?

David was still puzzling over the question as they approached the open doors of the chapel, through which could be heard the majestic swell of an organ, accompanying the well-trained student chorus. Though he didn't recognize the song, he was stirred by the beauty of the music.

The boys stood at the front of the chapel, just to

the right of the pulpit. In perfect unison, they sang out:

Hail the powers of Jesus' name! Let angels prostrate fall.
Bring forth the royal diadem, and crown Him Lord of all!

Listening more carefully now to the lyrics, David realized that the choir was singing a Christian hymn much like the Christmas songs he'd learned in school chorus.

Once inside the chapel Reece, Dillon, and Van Kelt broke away from the rest of the group and headed toward the front. Unsure whether he should follow them, David opted instead to stick with Connors, McGivern, and the others. He followed them down the center aisle as they filed into one of the straight-back pews.

Each of the boys was holding what appeared to be a prayer book. David removed one from the back of the seat in front of him and peeked at McGivern's to see what page they were on. McGivern rolled his eyes and nodded toward Connors, on his other side, who was singing along enthusiastically but noticeably off-key.

There was an almost palpable sense of order and well-being in the chapel sanctuary. The rows were filled with handsome, healthy-looking boys, all of whom seemed to exude an aura of superiority and prestige. It was as if by virtue of their enrollment at St. Matthew's they were members-in-training of a rigorously exclusive club that admitted to its elite

ranks only the smartest, strongest, and bravest of
lboys.

Though David doubted that he could have put
his feelings into words, he was beginning to understand what his father and Coach McDevitt had
been trying to tell him: These boys were privileged
because they'd been born into the right families.
Now it was *his* privilege to spend this year among
them, surrounded by America's future politicians
and business executives, its college professors and
university presidents.

If he were lucky enough that even just a little of
their polish rubbed off on him, he would have a
chance to live a far different life than his parents
and grandparents had. The growing awareness of
that possibility was both exciting and disturbing.

Now the choir was jubilantly completing the last
verse of the hymn:

> For still our ancient foe
> Doth seek to work us woe.
> His craft and power are great,
> And armed with cruel hate
> On earth is not his equal.

David joined in the concluding "Amen." Four
hundred hymnals snapped shut. Four hundred boys
took their seats. A white-haired man of about sixty,
who stood tall and straight as a drill sergeant,
strode up to the lectern and scrutinized his congregation. Behind him, David noticed, were seated
Reece, Dillon, and Van Kelt, as well as three other
students whom he hadn't yet met. All six boys were

wearing brocade satin vests in red and blue, the school colors.

Suddenly he remembered another piece of information from the school catalogue. Each year six boys were honored for their scholastic and athletic achievements by being chosen to serve as the senior prefects. The prefects were supposed to set the standard of excellence for the rest of the St. Matthew's students. So Dillon hadn't been joking when he'd said that he and his friends were the big men on campus. David figured he was pretty lucky to have been accepted into this group.

But before he had much chance to dwell on this thought the white-haired man began to speak. His voice boomed out across the chapel like a deep, rolling clap of thunder.

"Gentlemen of St. Matthew's, welcome to the finest preparatory school in the nation," he declared. "Welcome especially to our new boys. I am Dr. Bartram, your headmaster. The rest of you may conceivably remember me."

The audience rustled with laughter.

"The annual joke. Make the most of it," Connors muttered under his breath to David.

"Tomorrow begins the one hundred and ninety-third fall term—"

"—And no," Connors whispered, matching Dr. Bartram word for word, "I was *not* in office when the first one began."

David couldn't help but smile at Connors's nervy humor as the headmaster continued. "Nor shall I be in office, I sincerely trust, when and if the last term begins. We are part of a continuum, a process that has neither beginning nor end, yet has both origins and purpose. The things you learn here, the values you adopt, will stay with you for the rest of your life."

Many of the boys were stifling yawns as they struggled to pay attention to much the same speech Dr. Bartram gave every September. David, however, listened closely, following every word as if it might hold the key to his success at St. Matthew's.

Dr. Bartram leaned forward above the podium and gazed intently at his charges. He said, "Some of you new boys may find that academics and discipline at St. Matthew's are very demanding. I will point out that much of what is policy here, including our cherished honor code, has been established not by me or by your teachers, but by your fellow students—to be enforced by your own tribunal of prefects—as it has been for the last two centuries."

He paused and indicated with a wave of his hand the six boys sitting behind him. Then he went on, "We judge ourselves here, and we judge ourselves by the highest standards. You are, my boys, among the elite of the nation, and we seek here at St. Matthew's to prepare you for the heavy responsibility that comes with favored position. Today more than ever this country needs an elite that cares more for honor than for advantage, more for service than for personal gain. To that end, let us beseech the help of God, in Whose name we pray."

Everyone present bowed heads—all except for David, who looked around, momentarily confused.

SCHOOL TIES

"Our Father, Who art in heaven, hallowed be Thy name," Dr. Bartram intoned.

The words had a strange, unfamiliar ring to David, who was used to hearing prayers spoken only in Hebrew. Stranger still was the practice of bowing his head. At synagogue there were two or three moments during the service when worshipers bent their knees slightly and bowed as a sign of respect. Here, however, he was obviously expected to follow Christian custom, and the gesture came less easily than he might have anticipated.

". . . Thy will be done, on earth as it is in heaven. . . ."

David took one last look at the sea of bowed heads and thought about all the Christmas carols he had sung without caring that Christmas wasn't a Jewish holiday. Then he, too, bowed his head and joined the rest of the students and staff as Dr. Bartram led them in a recitation of the Lord's Prayer.

57

4

St. Matthew's students were expected to adhere to a rigid schedule. Dinner was served at seven o'clock sharp, and nobody was excused without a signed note from his housemaster. After dinner the boys had two hours of supervised study hall followed by a half hour of free time before the strictly enforced lights out at eleven.

On this first night of school the boys were allowed the luxury of two extra free hours to unpack and get their rooms in order. But before David had even filled the top drawer of his dresser with socks and underwear, Reece was urging him to come and listen to McGivern's newly purchased stack of rock 'n' roll records.

David happily shoved his duffel bag into the closet and followed his roommate across the hall. The other six boys had already made themselves comfortable in McGivern and Connors's room.

They lay across the beds and on the floor, snapping their fingers, tapping their feet, and singing along to the raucous rhythms of "Smokey Joe's Café."

"Decent hi-fi, Mac," Van Kelt drawled as he strummed an imaginary guitar.

McGivern moved over to make room for David on the bed and pushed a box of cookies toward him. "Bought it this summer from a friend back home," he said.

"How much?"

"He wanted forty bucks, but I jewed him down to thirty."

Reaching for another cookie, David felt his hand freeze in midair. He glanced at Reece, then at Connors, wondering which of them would be the first to slam McGivern for his lousy choice of words. But they as well as the rest of the group were behaving as if nothing had happened.

"I'll give you twenty-five for it," Van Kelt offered McGivern.

David *knew* he couldn't have been the only one in the room to have heard McGivern's slur. If someone in Scranton had dared to use that same expression, Bear would have socked him so hard and fast that the guy would have been flat on his face before he had time to blink. But here nobody seemed even the slightest bit disturbed by the comment.

"Look at him, always trying to get something for nothing," Dillon was saying, pointing at Van Kelt.

"And he's not even Jewish," shouted Magoo.

His insight provoked a round of applause.

David's heart was pounding like a sledgehammer. He felt as if he were in the middle of a bad dream, and there was no way to wake up from it. The boys seemed like a good bunch of guys, not the type to be deliberately cruel or nasty. They had gone out of their way to make him a part of their group. David knew lots of guys who wouldn't have done the same. Yet none of them seemed to give a damn that they'd insulted him.

Unless—was it possible?—they didn't know he was Jewish. And how or why *would* they have known, unless someone had told them? He didn't look particularly Jewish, whatever that meant. And the name Greene wasn't like Cohen or Goldberg— instantly identifiable as being Jewish.

Coach McDevitt had advised him to keep his cards close to his vest. Now David wondered whether the coach had meant that he should keep his mouth shut about his religion.

A young man who looked like he'd only recently graduated from college knocked on the open door and stepped into the room. He was carrying a pipe and wearing a black sweater with the orange Princeton logo emblazoned across the front. "Evening, gentlemen," he greeted them.

"Evening," the boys said.

He gestured with his pipe toward the record player. "Whose music is that, and I use the term advisedly?" he asked, shouting to be heard above the noise.

"That's the immortal Robins," Connors informed him, sounding somewhat astonished that there might be any doubt as to who the singers were.

"No, I mean the man who would purchase such swill."

The boys exchanged amused glances. Who was this creep anyway?

"That would be me," McGivern admitted with a sly grin. He winked at Connors, as if to say, Watch me have some fun with this asshole.

"That would be *I*," the fellow corrected him. "Have you a name?"

"McGivern. And you?"

"Mr. Cleary," the man said, drawing on his pipe. "I happen to be the new housemaster."

The group's high spirits were deflated as quickly as a pricked balloon. Even David, as inexperienced as he was in the ways of St. Matthew's, could begin to imagine the disadvantages of having Mr. Cleary as housemaster.

"The cultural environment in which one lives ought to be as important as the air he breathes and the food he eats," Mr. Cleary said, pronouncing his words as if his jaw were wired shut.

But McGivern, the son of a lawyer, knew his constitutional rights. What about his freedom to listen to the music of his choice? Grinning insolently, he silently challenged the housemaster to *make* him turn off the record.

Mr. Cleary was new to St. Matthew's and determined to establish himself as a fearsome disciplinarian. Otherwise, the headmaster had cautioned him when he'd been hired for the job, the boys would walk all over him. These uncivilized fellows represented the first challenge to his authority. He didn't dare lose the battle. He walked over to the record player, picked up the needle, and turned off the machine.

The room went silent. Mr. Cleary grasped the offending object between his fingertips and held it away from his body, behaving as if the record were emitting a foul odor.

But McGivern, never one to give up easily, said, "Surely in your day you had your own music, sir."

"Yes, and my day has not passed. David Brubeck, Ray Anthony, Les Elgart . . ." Mr. Cleary enumerated his musical preferences as he handed McGivern his record. Then he said, "We'll have no problem. Gentlemen, we all have to live here. Let's not bring the jungle into the house, shall we?"

He turned and strode toward the door.

Earlier, David had kept quiet. He hadn't been able to defend his own honor in the face of the boys' unwitting bigotry. But Mr. Cleary's reference to the jungle suddenly struck him as yet another bigoted dig, this one based on the color of the Robins' skin.

A mischievous demon seemed to have perched itself on his shoulder, goading him to take his anger out on the housemaster. He was just as surprised as the others when he opened his mouth and pierced the silence with a hyena's shrill screech.

Mr. Cleary whirled around. He glared at the eight innocent-looking faces struggling to maintain their composure, then turned again to go.

David let out a second piercing, monkeylike shriek. The boys could hardly contain themselves as Mr. Cleary glowered his displeasure. But he knew better than to try to pick out the guilty party. Determined to preserve what remained of his dignity, he stomped out of the room without another word.

The boys fell on the floor, hooting and shrieking and screaming with laughter.

"God, Greene," Magoo gasped. "Where'd you get the balls?"

Connors squinched up his eyes and pretended to grope his way blindly around the room. "Scranton, Magoo," he yelled. "That's like in America."

"You are *in*, David," Reece announced a few minutes later. They were back in their room, getting ready to go to sleep. Still chuckling, he stripped off his pants and dropped them on the floor of his closet.

"I hope all the teachers aren't like him," said David, shrugging off his jacket.

"Most of them are okay. Who'd you get for history?"

David consulted his class cards. "Gierasch," he said, unknotting his tie.

"A born killer. I got him, too. How about French?"

"Renard."

"Good. We'll get him talking about the French Resistance and catch up on our sleep," Reece declared. He threw on his robe and flung a towel over his shoulder. "Do you shower in the morning or night?"

"Night."

"Better hurry," Reece cautioned as he headed for the bathroom. "We'll just make it before lights out."

David nodded and unbuttoned his shirt. Opening his drawer to grab a washcloth, he caught a glimpse of himself in the mirror. Dangling from his neck on a long silver chain was his silver Star of David, a bar mitzvah present from his parents.

He hadn't taken it off since his parents had given it to him the night before he had been called up for the first time to read from the Torah. But now he wasted a few precious minutes before lights out to unclasp the chain and remove the necklace. He held it in the palm of his hand, closed his fist around it, and felt the sharp points of the six-sided star digging into his skin.

He unclenched his fist and slowly swung the chain back and forth in front of his eyes, like a hypnotist working with a reluctant subject. He wouldn't have been caught dead wearing any other jewelry. His Star of David, however, was different from a class ring or an ID bracelet. It was a reminder of how everyone had made such a fuss over him on his bar mitzvah day . . . how happy his parents had been . . . how proud he'd felt as he'd looked out at the congregation and delivered the speech that Grandpa had helped him write.

In Scranton, where lots of guys on the team wore crosses under their shirts, he'd thought of the star as just another good-luck charm that helped him win games and get good grades.

But the guys here at St. Matthew's might not

understand about good-luck charms. They were *born* lucky. He bet that none of them wore a cross around his neck or carried a rabbit's foot in his pocket.

No big deal, he thought as he pulled a Band-Aid box out of his drawer. He pushed and twisted the necklace until he managed to fit it inside the box. For safekeeping. Not because he was trying to hide it from anyone. He wasn't ashamed of his religion. No, sirree, he assured himself as he followed Reece to the bathroom. He wasn't trying to hide anything from anyone.

The next morning David woke up to a hard, steady rain that sent the leaves tumbling from the trees and swirling across the sidewalks. Magoo and Dillon grumbled through breakfast about the lousy weather. But as they all trooped off to their first class of the day in Emerson Hall David couldn't help but notice that even under a gunmetal-gray sky the campus was one of the prettiest places he had ever seen. He felt as if he had stepped into an English movie, where the masters treated their students with utmost respect and talked philosophy with them over tea and biscuits.

The fantasy passed the moment his group walked into French class and discovered there'd been a change in their schedules.

"Well, well," declared Mr. Cleary. "My musical upstairs neighbors." He had exchanged his Princeton sweater for a tweed jacket, and the pipe was missing from his mouth. But otherwise he seemed every bit as pompous and smug as he had the night before when he had complained about the rock 'n' roll.

"I'm dead," whispered McGivern as he slid into a seat at the back of the room.

"Monsieur Renard is cutting back on his teaching load, so I will have the pleasure of teaching this section of French Four," Mr. Cleary explained, grimly eying McGivern. *"Et celà, messieurs, est le dernier anglais que vous allez entendre pendant cette heure-ci. Ayant étudier français pour trois années, vous devriez pouvoir entretenir des conversations. N'est-ce pas, McGivern? Monsieur McGivern?"*

David struggled to keep up with Mr. Cleary's rapid-fire monologue. He managed to catch enough to understand that the teacher intended to speak only French for the rest of the hour, and that he expected his students to be able to converse in French as well. Uh-oh. He had gotten pretty good grades in French the last three years, but the emphasis had always been on reading and grammar, not conversation.

His only consolation was that McGivern also seemed to be having trouble following Mr. Cleary. He looked left and right, as if appealing for help, rolled his eyeballs heavenward, and chewed on his thumbnail. Finally he said, *"Oui, monsieur."*

"Oui, monsieur, quoi, McGivern?" asked Mr. Cleary.

"I'm sorry, sir." McGivern shook his head. "I don't understand."

"Français!" Mr. Cleary exhorted. *"Français!"*

McGivern's face flushed bright red, and he groped for the words to express that he could neither speak nor understand French. *"Je suis désolé, monsieur, mais je n'ai pas parle ni entendu le français. . . ."*

Mr. Cleary covered his ears as if it pained him to hear French spoken thus. *"Arretez! Arretez! C'est mutilation!"* He interrupted McGivern to brand his response a mutilation of the language.

A study in misery, McGivern sank low in his seat, pulled out his notebook, and ignored his friends' sympathetic glances.

Jeez, thought David. The first minute of his first class, and he was already wondering whether he could stick out the year. Making friends was no sweat. The guys were great. But making the grade could be a hell of a lot tougher than he had counted on.

To David's great relief, the rest of his classes proved to be far less traumatic than French. Even Mr. Gierasch, the history teacher whom Reece had described as "a born killer," seemed tame in comparison with Mr. Cleary. By the end of his sixth and final class of the day David had realized that it would take some extra work on his part to catch up in French and calculus. But he knew he could manage so long as he put in the time studying— and he was determined not to fail, no matter how long he had to sit on his butt with his nose stuck in a book.

He had been counting the hours until football practice. He was itching to get out on the field, run laps, let loose the load of nervous energy that had been building in him since the morning. However behind he might be academically, he knew that out there on the field he could hold his own against any one of his teammates.

The cast of characters assembled in the locker room was different from what he was used to. But the sounds and odors were the same. A gym, no matter how plain or fancy the building, always smelled of dirty socks and jockstraps, of sweat and hair grease and boys trying to prove themselves to their peers.

He was heartened by the familiar noises—and pleased to discover that even at St. Matthew's, boys fooled around behind the coach's back, snapping towels and yelling good-natured insults at each other. These guys were no angels, even if they were, to quote Dr. Bartram, among the nation's elite.

McGivern, dressed in his Shadow costume, had apparently recovered from Mr. Cleary's assault on his dignity. He and another student were passing out gear and uniforms to the players. As David went to try his on for size Coach McDevitt waved hello to him. David waved back but didn't stop to talk, because he saw that Coach had pulled Dillon aside for a private conference.

"I don't have to tell you how a team works, do I?" the coach was saying to Dillon.

"I get the picture, Coach," said Dillon, struggling to keep the resentment out of his voice. "I wasn't the quarterback you were looking for."

"You're still our number one backup," Coach McDevitt promised him.

Backup meant second best, and second best was unacceptable in the Dillon family. But Dillon knew better than to try and explain that to the coach, who didn't come from the kind of background where people were expected to win the gold medal, and nobody got any points for being the runner-up.

Nor did he want the coach—or anyone else, for that matter—to know how much it hurt to see Greene grab his spot. Trying to sound philosophical, Dillon said, "But if I want to play, I better play halfback."

"That's our weakest spot now," the coach reminded him. "You'll make a great halfback, you got the stuff. Just work on the blocks, the running."

Bullshit, thought Dillon. He'd make a much better quarterback than a halfback. Greene would never be able to hold up under all the pressure. Maybe he could score some points at his diddlysquat public school in Pennsylvania. But here in Massachusetts, where the big boys played, he would very quickly be shown up for the second-stringer that Dillon knew he had to be. Then Dillon would get his spot back, and everyone would be happy again.

And in the meantime . . .

"I'll give it my best," he told Coach McDevitt.

The coach nodded approvingly. This was just what he wanted to hear from Dillon. He said, "I'm counting on it." Then, moving to the center of the room, he cupped his hands together and roared, "Listen up!"

The room went instantly quiet.

"New face in the varsity this year." Coach told

the group what most of them already knew. "David Greene."

All eyes turned toward David, who self-consciously busied himself with his cleats.

"Greene comes to us from Pennsylvania," Coach continued. "Plays quarterback. Led his team to a league championship last year, and it was a mighty tough league. So this year we're gonna work on a passing game. McGivern's gonna give you some new plays."

McGivern, in his alter ego persona of the Shadow, slunk through the group, doling out the mimeographed play sheets. "If captured, eat it. If you're still alive, meet here tomorrow," he whispered furtively.

Nobody paid any attention to McGivern's act. They were all so used to his antics that they ignored his odd behavior. Even Coach McDevitt took it for granted. "Study 'em tonight," he instructed the boys. "We'll run through 'em tomorrow. Today let's go out and warm up. Hit it!"

The coach spent the first few minutes of practice dividing the team into squads to run the various drills. David was assigned to work out with Reece, Van Kelt, and Terry, a center who lived in another dorm. The grass was wet and slippery from the rain that had finally stopped just before sixth period. But when David trotted onto the field and got his first look at the regulation-sized, hundred-yard rectangle, he felt like a little kid who had just been handed the key to the candy store.

The turf was perfectly groomed; the tiered rows

of bleachers rose high on three sides as witness to the interest and affluence of the St. Matthew's alumni; the goalposts and scoreboard were freshly painted a deep, dark green that shone through the gloom of the cloudy autumn twilight.

Dillon, Connors, and a couple of other halfbacks were taking turns attempting to dodge the defensive linemen. Connors feinted right, but either he was too slow or the boys on the defensive line were too agile. A burly linebacker stopped him dead before he got a chance to gain any yardage.

"Read it and weep, Dillon. Life as you know it has changed," Connors hooted as he ambled past his disconsolate friend.

In the meantime, Van Kelt and Reece had run out to wait for the pass. David lined up behind Terry, who spun the ball between his legs in a short, hard snap. David grabbed hold of the brown pigskin and sent it flying toward his teammates at the thirty-yard line. The ball lofted high and long before it neatly dropped into Van Kelt's waiting hands.

Van Kelt and Reece sprinted downfield, tossing the ball back and forth before they returned it to Terry.

"This guy is good," shouted Van Kelt. "He could hit a dime."

Reece raised his fingers in a V-for-victory sign. He was beginning to believe that this could be a much different year for the boys of St. Matthew's.

Coach McDevitt wasn't the only member of the staff who was observing the practice. Dr. Bartram and Mr. Pierce, the chaplain, had also stopped by to have a look at the team. Though David would have had no way of knowing it, they were primarily interested in his performance.

"He does have an arm," Mr. Pierce acknowledged as David let rip a series of tightly wound passes.

Dr. Bartram watched Reece leap into the air to capture the ball. "I can't help wondering," he said, shaking his head, "if we've done the right thing."

"Yes, I know. But it's too late now," Mr. Pierce reminded him.

The headmaster sighed deeply. "To break nearly two centuries of tradition just to beat St. Luke's . . . No sports rivalry is worth doing this."

He shook his head and turned away, too distressed by the change to make his peace with David Greene's presence on the field.

The previous evening a picniclike atmosphere had prevailed at dinner. The hamburgers, cheese-grilled frankfurters, and mashed potatoes had been set out buffet-style on two long tables, from which the boys had helped themselves until the food ran out. Normally, however, dinner was a formal, sit-down affair at which the boys were required to wear jackets and ties. They were also expected to mind their manners: no elbows on the tables; cloth napkins spread across their laps where they belonged; no eating until after grace was recited by a housemaster or one of the prefects.

Of course, Reece, Dillon, and the rest of the gang always sat together. The underclassmen, who treated them with the respect they deserved as big men on campus, moved quickly out of their way as the boys strolled through the dining room toward their table.

One of the tenth graders, whose parents owned a summer home in Maine next door to Dillon's, decided to show off for his friends. "Hi, Dillon!" he piped up, playing on the family connection. "How was practice?"

Connors chortled but managed to keep his mouth shut. Dillon, still hurting from the disastrous practice he had just endured, glared at the younger boy until he realized that the kid had intended no harm by his question. He was staring up at Dillon with the big, hungry eyes of a faithful puppy dog yearning for an approving pat on the head.

Dillon winked at the tenth grader. Then he stuck two fingers into the boy's water glass, withdrew his hand, and flicked water all over his face. As he sauntered away the boy was drying his face with his napkin and grinning with the pleasure of having been noticed by one of the big shots.

In order to create more of a family feeling, a faculty member or his wife was assigned to sit at the head of each of the tables. The table that Dillon and his pals had claimed as their own was presided over by Mr. Swanson, an English teacher who had the earnest, troubled blue eyes of a poet and a pale complexion that was easily provoked to a blush. He was already seated, as were the other boys, when Dillon took his place. One chair was still empty.

"Where's Greene?" asked Van Kelt, feeling it his duty to save the last seat for David.

Reece reached for the water pitcher. "I don't know," he said, filling his glass. "He was gone when I got back from the library. I thought he'd be here."

"Save a place for him," said Van Kelt.

Reece looked around the room, wondering what was keeping his roommate. It would be too bad if David was late, because Mr. Swanson could be a real stickler about tardiness. Besides, to judge from the aromas wafting in from the kitchen, the cook had made pork chops and fried potatoes, one of his better meals. After two hours of football drills Reece was starving. He imagined that Greene must be, too.

Wishing that the headmaster would arrive so Mr. Pierce could say grace, Reece glanced restlessly toward the kitchen door, where the student waiters were already lined up, ready to begin serving. Astonished, he took a second, harder look. Then he gave Dillon a poke in the ribs with his elbow and nodded in the direction of the kitchen. There stood his absent roommate, holding a silver tray and outfitted like the rest of the waiters in a spotless white jacket.

So Greene had to earn himself some pocket money by waiting on tables. Reece knew he should have figured from the way Greene dressed that his family wasn't exactly rolling in dough. And he had, after all, been awarded an alumni scholarship. Still, Reece felt bad for Greene. He had a heavy load to juggle, what with having to work in the dining room, keep up his grades, and attend football practice every afternoon.

Dillon, on the other hand, was wasting no pity on

his rival for the quarterback position. In fact, he was able to smile for the first time since the coach had pulled him aside earlier that afternoon to give him the bad news.

Well, well . . . Here was information that put a whole new light on the subject of David Greene. So what if he had impressed McDevitt with a couple of lucky throws? The guy was a poverty case. He came from a damned public school in Scranton, Pa., for shit's sake. When he opened his mouth he sounded like a turkey. He didn't belong at St. Matthew's. Any fool could see the truth. David Greene just wasn't one of them.

A smirk played across Dillon's lips as Dr. Bartram strode through the room. The headmaster took his place between the chaplain and the senior master at the head table, which stood on a raised platform at the far end. Mr. Pierce rose and bowed his head. Everyone, including David, did likewise.

"Thank You, dear God, for Your bountiful gifts that we are about to receive," the chaplain declared. "Thank You for the wonders of nature and the joys of friendship. In the name of Thy Son, Jesus Christ, amen."

This time David didn't stop to think about whether or not to bow his head. Nor did he waste even a second wondering whether it was okay for him to say "amen" after a prayer that sounded so different from his own. After only one full day on campus he understood what was demanded of a St. Matthew's student. He was expected to live up to the school's exacting standards. He was expected to make sure that his team outscored the opposition, especially when they played St. Luke's. Most importantly, he was expected to behave as if he, too, had been groomed from birth to fit in at St. Matthew's.

Indian summer had come to Massachusetts. The leaves on the trees that shaded the campus were just beginning to change from deep green to their autumnal palette. But the warm sun and soaring temperatures felt more like July than September, and the scent of fresh-cut grass only added to the illusion. To make matters worse, Mr. Gierasch had decided to spring a surprise quiz on his seniors, who sat fidgeting in their seats, trying to ignore the buzz of the lawnmower just outside the open classroom window.

Exhausted by the heat, Mr. Gierasch's dog, an ancient, weary English corgi, lay snuffling in his sleep next to his master's desk. Mr. Gierasch paced the classroom, slapping a ruler against the palm of his hand for emphasis as he peppered his students with names and dates out of English history.

He stopped and peered over Connors's shoulder. "Henry the Eighth assumes throne."

Connors took a lucky guess. "1509," he answered, breathing a sigh of relief as the teacher moved on.

"Same Henry concocts Church of England," Gierasch demanded.

"1534," Van Kelt said quickly.

Gierasch took a few steps and turned to find his next victim. "Mr. Smith? 1649."

"Charles the First was executed?" replied

Chesty, whose hands were wrapped around the sides of his desk, as if to help him keep his balance.

"Correct." Mr. Gierasch glared at Connors for no reason that the boy could figure out. "Which resulted in the establishment of . . ." He pointed his ruler at Van Kelt.

An easy one. "A commonwealth, Mr. Gierasch, sir."

"Very good," Mr. Gierasch loudly declared.

The corgi's ears twitched as he shifted his position, but he didn't wake up. After so many years of attending classes he was used to the rapid tempo of his master's quizzes.

The teacher whirled around and leaned forward across Dillon's desk. "Mr. Dillon," he barked. "When did Mary, Queen of Scots, lose her head?"

Dillon had been daydreaming about swimming off the dock in Maine. Summoned back to the present, he furrowed his brow and took a stab at an answer. "1687," he said, trying to sound convinced.

"Close." Mr. Gierasch whacked his ruler against Dillon's desk. "You're only a century off. Mr. Greene?"

"1587," said David, grateful for the hint.

"Indeed. And what occurred during the years 1553 to 1558? Mr. Collins?"

"That was the reign of Bloody Mary Tudor," said Magoo.

"So it was. Which resulted in what, Mr. Greene?"

Caught off-guard, David swallowed a yawn and straightened his tie as he stalled for time. Then he remembered. "Persecution of the Protestants. Catholicism was restored."

"How come, Mr. Connors?"

"She married what's his name," Connors stammered, wishing Gierasch would get off his back. "Philip."

"More or less," Mr. Gierasch conceded. "August 9, 1593. Anybody?"

Fifteen pairs of eyes stared back at him blankly.

"The birth of Izaak Walton. A personal favorite." Mr. Gierasch chuckled. He liked to keep the boys on their toes by throwing out the name of a writer or artist who wasn't otherwise included in the curriculum.

Dillon glanced at David. *"Who?"* he mouthed. David shrugged. He had never heard of the guy.

"Mr. Dillon," said Mr. Gierasch, rocking back on his heels. "A literary event. 1611?"

Dillon tried but failed to retrieve the answer from his memory.

"McGivern?"

"Publication of the King James Bible," McGivern glibly replied.

"Correct. Care to try for three, Mr. Dillon?" asked Mr. Gierasch. Noting the boy's grimace, he added, "I remind you, Mr. Dillon, this course has no shallow end. Sink or swim."

Dillon was literally saved by the ringing of the class bell, which put an abrupt end to Mr. Gierasch's lecture. The corgi raised his head, stretched, and followed the boys with his eyes as they hurried out of the room.

"A hundred pages of Morrison's thorough and

excruciatingly straightforward text for tomorrow," Mr. Gierasch called after them. "Yes, indeed, Mr. Dillon. Tomorrow is that day which directly follows today."

"This is true," Van Kelt seconded him.

Dillon groaned. First the coach, now Gierasch. The way these bastards were picking on him, he didn't know how the heck he would get through the next nine months.

David's father had made him promise to call home once a week. Yes, of course, it would be cheaper if David wrote letters, Pop had agreed. But he knew how busy David would be, how easily he could forget to drop a line or two. So the bill would be a few more dollars than usual. He wanted to stay in touch with his son. Wanted to know how David was making out at St. Matthew's. Was he making friends with the other boys? Feeling okay about the team? Doing all right with his schoolwork? "Keeping up," David told him. "Holding my own."

"How about French?" asked Pop.

Hunched over the receiver in the hall pay phone, David made a face. Trust Pop to hit on his worst subject. How did he know him so well? "I hate the teacher."

"Everybody hates at least one of 'em," Pop reassured him. "Don't let it bother you."

"Yeah," said David noncommittally, eager to be done with the conversation. It was too hot in the phone booth to close the door, and he hated the lack of privacy.

Besides, talking to Pop reminded David how

much he missed everyone. He didn't want to feel homesick. It seemed like a waste of time. All this week he had succeeded in blocking out any memories of the people he had left behind in Scranton. Now he found himself thinking about his sister and brother, about Bear, Nick, Annette, Joyce, and the rest of the gang.

"I'd better get back to the books," he said. "I'll call you next week."

"Okay, back to work," Pop agreed, though he sounded like he might have wanted to stay on longer. Then he added, "Don't forget about Saturday."

"Saturday . . ." David tried to recall what was special about the day. Was it Sarah or Petey's birthday? Should he have sent a card?

"It's Rosh Hashanah. You didn't forget," Pop said in a tone of voice that was midway between a question and an accusation.

Shit. He had completely forgotten about the Jewish new year, which his family always celebrated together. It was Pop's fault for not having mentioned it earlier, he told himself, feeling unaccountably guilty. The Jewish holidays were hard to keep track of, because every year they fell on different days . . . sometimes even different months.

Saturday. "I've got a game against Winchester, Pop," he said. This time it was his tone of voice that wavered between a question and a statement.

"It's a very holy day, Davy," his father interrupted him. "And it goes back a lot longer than any of us. You show respect and get to the synagogue."

Glad that his father wasn't there to see him, David made a face. What a joke. Nobody had ever said anything about there being a synagogue on the campus. David doubted very much that he would find a synagogue in town. But even if one did exist, students weren't allowed off campus without special permission from the headmaster.

"Okay, sure," he said, figuring that what Pop didn't know would never hurt him. "Don't worry. Speak to you next week."

He banged down the receiver and slumped against the back of the booth. If Rosh Hashanah went back so many centuries, what difference could it possibly make if one guy out of all the millions of Jews in the world skipped the holiday just this one year?

Didn't Pop get it? David couldn't miss the very first game of the season. His teammates would never forgive him. Well, probably Dillon would forgive him, because then he could play quarterback. But Coach McDevitt and the rest of the guys would think he'd gone nuts if he suddenly announced he had something more important to do than face Winchester on Saturday.

He would say an extra prayer—a Jewish prayer—in chapel on Sunday. God would understand, even if his father couldn't.

5

The St. Matthew's boys were having a terrible day. Coach McDevitt stared in disbelief as Reece, his best wide receiver, took a hit from the Winchester team and tumbled to the ground at the six-yard line. He rubbed his hand along his chin, popped another digestive mint in his mouth, and gritted his teeth to stop himself from swearing.

His boys were playing like a bunch of ten-year-olds who didn't know their asses from their elbows about the game of football. Nothing was going right for them. They weren't completing their passes. They weren't gaining any yardage. His quarterback was behaving as if the ball were a red-hot potato, and all he could think to do was fling it in the air to get rid of it.

McDevitt was baffled. Greene had been looking great in practice. He was a smart kid with a dynamite arm and a good head for calling clever plays. Why this afternoon did he look like he'd never handled a football before in his life?

Nerves. It was the only explanation that made any sense. The coach could have kicked himself for not seeing it sooner. All this talk about how Greene was a special case because he'd entered as a senior on an alumni scholarship . . . that was a heavy load to shoulder. The kid was under a heck of a lot of pressure. He had to be made to understand—it was only a game.

Coach McDevitt made a T with his hands, signaling for a time out, and gestured to David that he wanted to talk.

David jogged over to join him on the side. "I'm sorry, Coach," he said, shaking his head. "I don't know what's wrong."

He was mortified by his performance on the field. He half expected the coach to kick him off the team right then and there. He deserved to be sent back to Scranton in disgrace. He held his breath, waiting for the inevitable scolding.

His coach surprised him. "Relax," he said. "Don't force it. Go out and have some fun."

Those were just about the last words David had figured to hear from Coach McDevitt. But Coach was right. David knew enough about his game to realize that his problem was mental, not physical. He had lost the natural, easy rhythm that normally drove his eye and arm the minute he stepped onto the field and started to call the plays. He was thinking too hard about all the people who were depending on him not to disappoint them: Reece, Van Kelt, and the rest of the guys. Coach McDevitt and Dr. Bartram. Pop back home in Scranton.

He was working too hard at trying to win. Today's game was like any other he had played over the course of his high school career. Only the faces and uniforms were different.

He gave Coach a nod to show he appreciated the vote of confidence, and McDevitt patted him on the fanny.

Calm down, David told himself as he ran back onto the field. Forget about trying to prove anything. Focus on having a good time.

The referee blew his whistle, and play resumed. David positioned himself behind his center at the line of scrimmage to wait for the snap. He stared across the field at Winchester's defensive line, shrugged off his worries, and decided to go with his pass play. Smiling behind the mouth guard of his helmet, he called the signals and dropped back six or seven feet into the pocket.

Van Kelt raced left in a cross-field pattern and found an empty hole. David fired him the ball. In one fluid motion he caught it against his chest, whirled around, and ran for the end zone. Three Winchester boys took him down, but not before he'd made a forty-yard gain.

The St. Matthew's fans cheered and clapped. Van Kelt brushed himself off, and David trotted downfield for the next play.

Dr. Bartram and Mr. Pierce were seated in the stands, watching the game in the company of their colleagues from Winchester. "That boy's very good," said Dr. Starley, pointing toward the field with his binoculars. "What's his name?"

"Van Kelt. The boys call him Rip. He's the team captain," Dr. Bartram told the Winchester headmaster, who had been a classmate of his at Harvard.

Mr. Pierce had overheard their exchange. Leaning forward, he said quietly, "I believe he means the boy who *threw* the pass, Dr. Bartram."

The headmaster frowned. He didn't appreciate being publicly corrected, especially by the chaplain. "Oh," he said sourly. "That's David Greene."

The second and third quarters were a blur of balls flying and bodies tumbling as the St. Matthew's players fought to regain the ground they had lost early in the game. But for all their efforts, they were still trailing twenty-one to twenty in the last minute and a half of the fourth quarter.

David felt as if his blood was on fire. He had totally lost track of his surroundings. All that existed for him was the ball, the field, and the outstretched hands of his wide ends. He waited for the center to hike him the ball on the twenty-five-yard line and scanned the defensive line.

"Down . . . hut one . . . hut two," he shouted.

He took the snap and faked a handoff to Dillon, who covered only a couple of feet before he plowed into a wall of Winchester bodies. Clutching the ball, David spun around and bolted toward the sideline. Still uncovered, he reversed directions and found enough room to run. He managed to make the first down before three Winchester players hurled themselves at him like a flying wedge and sent him crashing to the ground.

He hit the dirt and let go of the ball. But his opponents were bent on punishment. Two of them pinned David to the ground and formed a shield as the third smashed his fist into David's collarbone.

David yelped in pain and wrenched himself free. He didn't stop to think before he launched a counterattack with one swift, well-aimed jab of his knee. Then he scrambled to his feet and walked away without a backward glance, thereby missing the sight of his Winchester tormentor limping off the field with his hands cupped around his crotch.

A tumultuous roar went up from the St. Matthew's side. Dr. Starley and his chaplain pursed their lips in silent condemnation. Dr. Bartram likewise remained silent, but the look on his face conveyed his disapproval. "It is more blessed to give than to receive," murmured Mr. Pierce, who years earlier had been a scholarship student himself.

There were fifty-five seconds left to play. David took the snap, scrambled to make the throw, but couldn't find anyone who had even a chance of catching the pass. With no other option, he ran with the ball himself and gained a few yards before being called out of bounds.

The clock was stopped. The teams went into their huddles.

Mr. Pierce glanced at Dr. Bartram, who appeared to be displeased by David's accomplishments. Was he right in feeling that the headmaster seemed almost eager to witness a loss for his team?

Twenty-three seconds left on the clock. St. Matthew's was still trailing by one point. David called the signals. "Down . . . hut one, hut two, hut three . . ."

The center snapped the ball. The offensive line exploded forward. David scrambled back, looking for the open receiver. The clock was ticking down. Less than ten seconds remained of play. A second glance downfield, and David found what he'd been hoping to see. Reece had sneaked right and claimed a corner just shy of the end zone.

David drew a breath, aimed, and threw the pass to Reece. Students and teachers from both schools rose to their feet to follow its progress.

Outlined against the clear blue sky, the ball soared through the crisp fall air. Its trajectory formed a perfect arc as it spiraled higher and higher above the field, then commenced its descent into Reece's waiting hands. He stepped left to fake out the tackle. Then he whipped past him and dived for the end zone.

Touchdown!

Pandemonium erupted. The St. Matthew's boys screamed themselves hoarse and stomped their feet over David's performance. Reece, the game's other hero, met David midfield and tackled him in a celebratory hug. Moments later their teammates were all over them, pounding one another on the back and shouting their excitement.

Dr. Bartram accepted Dr. Starley's congratulations with a look that suggested something he had eaten for lunch hadn't quite agreed with him.

Coach McDevitt, on the other hand, was grinning like a Halloween jack-o'-lantern. "That's a goddamn ballplayer," he gleefully informed McGivern. "We're going to kick St. Luke's butt."

Perhaps because he had no relatives except for a sister who lived in Michigan, Dr. Bartram looked upon the St. Matthew's community—past and present—as his family. He took such a proprietary view of the school that he often conducted his own private tour of the grounds after lights out to ensure that all was in order.

On the evening following the St. Matthew's victory over Winchester Dr. Bartram was returning home from a dinner party hosted by Mr. Gierasch. The headmaster's earlier bad mood had been dispelled by the good food, fine wine, and excellent conversation served up at Mr. Gierasch's table.

As he strolled across the campus he pondered the validity of what his host and the other guests had said. Maintaining tradition was not to be scoffed at. Keeping the alumni happy, however, was equally important. And the alumni were as greedy as they were generous. They longed for triumphs on the football field to uphold St. Matthew's reputation as first among the best.

Without alumni contributions and endowments, St. Matthew's would be just another impoverished prep school struggling to pay its bills. Dr. Bartram decided that perhaps his friends were right. Admitting a boy named Greene who could lead their students to victory was a small price to pay.

Satisfied with that equation, the headmaster savored the nocturnal calm and order of his surroundings. To his left, the academic buildings stood dark and quiet. To his right, the lights in the dormitories were winking out one by one as the housemasters enforced the curfew.

Dr. Bartram inhaled the cool night air and bent to pick up a scrap of paper that had snagged on a bush. Straightening up, he was startled by the beam of light streaming through the chapel window.

Had Mr. Pierce forgotten to turn out the lights? Didn't the man realize that electricity was expensive? The headmaster shook his head over his chaplain's extravagance and turned down the path toward the chapel. As he approached the building it occurred to him that he might be about to catch an intruder in the midst of an act of vandalism.

Seated in the front row of the otherwise empty pews, David was too engrossed in private meditation to hear Dr. Bartram's footsteps as the headmaster cautiously tiptoed up the steps.

David had come to the chapel to pray. On his head was the yarmulke that Jewish men were required to wear in the synagogue. He had found it crumpled up in a corner of his duffel bag. Someone —his father or Sarah, perhaps—must have stuck it there without telling him. A few feet away, suspended above the altar, shone a large gilt cross. David wondered whether it was a sin for him to say his prayers in front of a cross. He had no choice, he decided. God would understand that.

"Shema Yisroel," he whispered, struggling to remember the Hebrew words. *"Adonai eloheinu, Adonai echad. Baruch shem k'vod malchuto leolam vaed.*

"Hear, O Israel, the Lord is our God, the Lord is One. Blessed be His glorious name forever and ever."

His Hebrew school teacher had said that the Shema was among the most important Jewish prayers because it affirmed the connection between God and the Jewish people. David figured it was the right one to say on Rosh Hashanah. Besides, he could remember only bits and pieces of the other ones he'd had to memorize for his bar mitzvah.

His concentration was broken by the sound of somebody's shoes slapping against the stone floor of the chapel. He stopped chanting and turned around.

"Who is it?" Dr. Bartram called out.

"David Greene, sir," he answered, whipping off his yarmulke and stuffing it in his pocket.

He hadn't been far from the truth, thought Dr. Bartram. If ever there was an intruder, it was the young man staring up at him with guilt-stricken eyes.

"What are you doing here, Greene?" the headmaster demanded.

"Praying, sir."

Dr. Bartram had heard a number of outrageous excuses in his day, but Greene's explanation had to win first prize for originality. Steepling his fingers, he said, "You realize the chapel is closed at this hour?"

"Does God have a closing time, sir?" David asked, surprising himself with his nerve. The smart-alecky question popped out of his mouth before he had a chance to think about what he was saying.

Dr. Bartram formed a smile that stopped at his lips. "I should imagine," he said, as if he were humoring David, "that your God allows prayer during daylight hours."

"I couldn't get away before now, sir. It's Rosh Hashanah, the beginning of the Jewish new year."

"I know what Rosh Hashanah is," the headmaster said, so obviously misstating the Hebrew words that David couldn't help but think his mispronunciation was deliberate. He cleared his throat and went on. "And it ends at sunset, if I recall the custom."

"Technically. But I didn't think it would go over too well if I said I couldn't play because of Rosh Hashanah." David paused to emphasize the correct pronunciation. "My scholarship depends on football."

An image came to Dr. Bartram's mind: The trustees' annual report, in which were listed the increases or decreases in donations for the previous fiscal year. The boy is serving a purpose here, he thought. It's my duty to humor him.

Aloud, he said dryly, "Yes, I saw the game. You seemed thoroughly concentrated on the task at hand."

"Thank you, sir."

The headmaster fixed his eyes on David and

studied him as if he were a rare specimen of insect, pinned and mounted for inspection. "You people are very . . . determined, aren't you?"

You people . . . Was he implying that David had been elected to represent the entire Jewish religion? Okay, he decided. If that was how Dr. Bartram needed to cast him, David would accept the role. "Sometimes we have to be, sir."

"I seem to recall a blessing. . . ." Dr. Bartram flicked an invisible speck of lint off his dinner jacket. " 'Blessed are the meek, for they shall inherit the earth.' "

It was the first David had heard of this particular blessing, but he wasn't about to admit that to the headmaster. "I wonder how meek they'll be when they do, sir," he said.

The whole concept sounded pretty dumb to him. The meek didn't win football games, which was supposed to be such a big deal here at St. Matthew's. So why was Dr. Bartram busting his ass? Pop probably would have gone for this meek stuff and told him to quit being such a wise guy. But Pop had also insisted he go to synagogue today. You couldn't have it both ways.

"Are you finished here, Mr. Greene?" asked Dr. Bartram.

"Yes, sir."

"Then I suggest you sneak back to your room," he said, looking past David's head. "I shall overlook this evening's infraction."

Feeling as if he had learned a lot more about the headmaster than he wanted to know, David stood up to leave.

The headmaster put out his hand to stop him. "Mr. Greene, was it worth it? Breaking a tradition just to win a football game?"

Now it was David's turn to stare at Dr. Bartram as if he were some sort of interesting specimen. Physically, the headmaster and Kocus couldn't have looked more different. But beneath the skin they both belonged to the same sorry species. Both of them were looking for a scapegoat. David wasn't volunteering for the job.

"Your tradition or mine, sir?" He threw his question to Dr. Bartram as deftly as he had thrown Reece the ball that had scored the winning touchdown. But this time he didn't stick around to celebrate his victory.

Monsieur Cleary, as the new French master insisted on being addressed, was fast winning himself the title of St. Matthew's least popular teacher. Even the best prepared, most confident students sweated through his daily drills and quizzes. For boys like McGivern and Dillon, who weren't particularly gifted at languages, his classes were a nightmare from which there was no escape.

"I can do French to English. The son of a bitch knows that, so he gives us English to French," grumbled McGivern, after yet another class during which he'd been made to look like a fool by Mr. Cleary's relentless needling.

The chiming of the bells, sonorously proclaiming the start of the next period, seemed to echo his growing sense that he was doomed to fail, no matter how hard he tried.

"That prick's not going to last here, I'll bet you anything," Connors said, trying to console him.

"He's not going to last?" McGivern shook his head and kicked at the fallen leaves that blanketed the sidewalk. "Connors, I flunked that test."

A group of boys was engaged in a spirited game of touch football in the middle of the campus. "You know, I'm getting sick and tired of these bells!" McGivern muttered, watching one of the boys lob the ball at the chaplain, who happened to be passing by.

Mr. Pierce had won letters for track and football while he was at prep school, and his arm still had some power behind it. He neatly fielded the ball, noticed Mr. Cleary walking purposefully toward the roadway, and tossed him a lateral pass that caught the French teacher by surprise.

Mr. Cleary put up his hands, but he was too late. The ball dropped to the ground. Reaching to grab for it, he accidentally kicked it instead and sent it spinning across the grass.

The boys guffawed at his clumsiness. Even Mr. Pierce couldn't hide his smirk. Mr. Cleary's know-it-all arrogance was winning him as few friends among the faculty as it was among his students.

Mr. Cleary glared at the players and continued on his way. Connors and McGivern saw him stop a few yards down in front of a 1950 MG roadster and possessively run his hand across the hood. Then he popped open the trunk, pulled out a can of wax and a cloth, and carefully began to apply the wax to the car's already gleaming surface. The boys exchanged knowing glances. It figured that Cleary would own an MG roadster, the Ivy Leaguer's ultimate status symbol.

The guy was not only a sadist, he was also a snob. McGivern groaned. What had he done to deserve this fate?

David had quickly discovered the value of yet another long-standing St. Matthew's tradition. The boys were encouraged to meet in small groups to review class notes and prepare for tests. The first time David sat down with his friends at one of the conference tables in the students' common room, he was amazed to see how much got accomplished. The boys took the sessions seriously, and there was very little fooling around.

With their books and papers spread out in front of them the boys tossed questions and answers at one another in a fast-moving game of verbal catch.

"So when James the Second was deposed . . ." said Van Kelt, challenging the others to jump in with the answer.

"William of Orange and Mary were crowned," Magoo said triumphantly.

"The Glorious Revolution. Why'd they call it that?" asked Connors.

Reece glanced up from his history text and looked around the table. "We scheduled this study group for Dillon's benefit," he pointed out. "The least he could do would be to show up."

McGivern yawned and hunched in his chair. "I checked his room. Maybe he's smoking in the butt room."

"I'll go get him," volunteered David, whose legs were stiff from sitting.

The walls of the corridor that led from the common room to the butt room—so named because it was the one place in the dorm where smoking was permitted—were hung with dour-faced portraits of prominent former residents of Iselin Hall. There was also a long bank of glass-fronted cabinets that held the hundreds of trophies awarded to generations of Iselin boys for their victories in intramural sports. Each trophy was engraved with the names of the players who had brought glory to their team and the year in which they had achieved that success.

David stopped in front of a display case and stared at its contents. In his spare moments, when he was alone as he was now, he had begun to play a game of sorts with himself—studying the names on the trophies, trying to find those that sounded even remotely Jewish. He had never given any thought before to the subject, and he wasn't sure which names qualified. A few came to mind: Rosen . . . Schwartz . . . Klein . . . Cohen . . . but what about Greene?

Never mind Greene, he thought. Where was Dillon? He headed quickly for the butt room but was distracted again by the sound of someone playing the piano. The musician, who wasn't just practicing scales, obviously knew how to coax real music out of the keyboard.

David followed the sounds to the music room and pushed open the door. The flames from the blaze in the fireplace threw flickering shadows across the leaded windows and oak bookshelves that lined the walls. Otherwise the huge room was dark except for one dim lamp perched atop the black grand piano. As David stepped closer to the piano he noticed a cigarette hanging from the edge of the keyboard, its lit tip glowing a bright red.

He stood quietly for a moment, waiting for Dillon to finish the phrase. Then he said, "I didn't know you could play. You're really good."

"I should work at a piano bar, huh?" said Dillon, puffing on his cigarette. "Screw college. Every night I could wear a tux and play in some smoky bar. Great-looking women would lean toward me with big tits hanging out and ask me to play. . . ." He trailed his hands along the keys and crooned, "Red sails in the sunset, way out on the sea . . ."

"Sounds good to me," said David, impressed by Dillon's expertise. "What about the study group?"

"Screw history." Dillon took another long drag, replaced the cigarette so that it dangled precariously off the edge, and resumed playing.

There were strict rules against smoking anywhere except in the butt room. David wondered why Dillon was taking such a chance—and why he was sounding so pissed off. He grabbed what was left of the cigarette, pinched the end until it was out, and dropped it in a wastebasket. Then he fanned away the cloud of smoke around Dillon's head.

"Will your parents be coming up for Homecoming?" Dillon asked, picking out a simple melody.

David sat down next to him on the piano bench

and noticed how effortlessly Dillon's fingers slid across the keyboard. "No," he said. "My father has to work."

"What about your mother?"

"She died three years ago. Leukemia."

"Jesus!" Dillon glanced at him sideways. "That's awful. Sorry, David."

David shrugged. Three years, and he still didn't know how to react when people expressed their condolences. It wasn't *their* fault his mother had died, so why did they feel they needed to apologize?

"My parents'll be here," Dillon went on. His fingers struck a dark, sad, minor-key chord. "My asshole brother will be here. Everybody will be here, waiting for Charlie to do something stupid."

"Like what?"

"I don't know. Sully the good name Dillon on the field of honor. You know about my brother and everything?"

"Sure." David quoted the line that inevitably followed any mention of Gray Dillon's name. "'The best quarterback St. Matt's ever had.'"

"Between you and me?" said Dillon, lowering his voice conspiratorially. "You're better. But he was good. I used to watch him play. I used to even be proud of him."

"Till when?"

"Till I started playing myself. Everybody kept expecting another Grayson Dillon the Third. Everybody kept getting disappointed. But hiding it very well, I must admit."

David thought about how hard Petey tried to be just like him. Petey imitated the way David walked, the way he combed his hair, the way he could polish off a quart of milk at one shot, straight from the container.

"Must be a bitch, being the kid brother," he said, his mind lingering on a memory of Petey posed in front of the mirror, his hands outstretched to grab the ball from his imaginary center. "Maybe that's why mine is always trying to kill me."

"Oh, I've had those thoughts." Dillon laughed, but he didn't seem all that amused.

"I know *one* song," said David.

Dillon chuckled again. This time the laughter sounded more genuine. "Let me guess," he said.

He plunked down one finger, then another, picking out "Chopsticks" like a child just learning to play. David jumped in with his two fingers. Dillon immediately cranked up the tempo so that David had to struggle to keep up with him. But he couldn't match Dillon's frantic, staccato rhythms. The guy was a demon at the piano. It was just too bad that he couldn't run downfield as fast as he could work the keyboard.

6

As the weeks passed David stopped wondering how things were going back home. St. Matthew's had become his school . . . his team . . . the place where he belonged. He quickly grew used to the exacting routine that ruled his day-to-day schedule: the long hours of classes; the mandatory study halls; most of all, the boisterous football practices where nothing less than a hundred percent was required on a daily basis.

Every Saturday afternoon the team took on its opposite number from yet another prep school. David had never encountered such brutal football. The competition within the prep school league was tough. The boys played to win—or maim. Bloody noses, broken fingers, and bruised ribs were all in an afternoon's work.

But with Reece and Van Kelt to back him up, David proved himself the key to the team's success.

As the St. Matthew's boys routed their foes from Connecticut all the way north to New Hampshire, Coach McDevitt took to bragging about David Greene's miracle arm, his agile way of dodging the linemen, his versatility and intelligence.

The home games were easier, of course, because they were played on familiar turf. But David especially looked forward to the away games, which gave him a chance to explore—at least through the window of the school bus—the panorama of the New England countryside.

By early October the leaves were splashed with the orange, magenta, and scarlet signatures of autumn. David was sure that the leaves changed colors in Pennsylvania, but he couldn't recall ever having seen such a display of so many brilliantly vivid shades.

The weather turned brisk and cold enough that the boys had to wear sweaters underneath their sports jackets. David could see his breath when he jogged around the quad before breakfast.

Bowls of tart McIntosh apples appeared on the tables alongside platters of pumpkin doughnuts and fresh apple cider, all sold cheaply at roadside stands near the campus. The boys were amused to discover that David had never tasted these treats before. What did people eat in Scranton, Pa.? Dillon asked with a wink.

David thought longingly of the chicken soup with matzo balls and sweet noodle puddings his mother had taught Sarah to make for dinner on Friday night. He thought about Mrs. Yacek's stuffed cabbage and the delicious smells that came from her kitchen when she fried up a batch of potato dumplings. But his friends seemed to enjoy the blandly roasted meat and potatoes, the veal chops served with mint jelly, the (horror of horrors) chipped beef on toast swimming in a cream sauce that was their typical fare in the dining room.

Gut instinct urged him to tell only half the truth. "We eat regular stuff," he responded to Dillon's question. "Tuna fish and hamburgers."

The next week there was almost a crisis over the cider. Van Kelt spotted several jugs of the thickly sweet drink, which had been disappearing from the kitchen at an alarming rate, wedged on the sill of Chesty's window. Chesty defended his right to store food in his room. But everyone knew that fermented cider could get you drunk. So Van Kelt, in his role as prefect, threatened to bring him before the honor board if he didn't return the jugs to the kitchen.

Chesty complied and knew he'd gotten off lucky. The long Columbus Day weekend was coming up. Nobody wanted to risk being grounded when the boys were scheduled to attend the first dance of the year.

After two months at an all-boys school, David was eager to meet the girls at the Overbrook School, St. Matthew's sister institution. His friends had variously described the girls as being "an okay bunch," "fun if you like dizzy blonds," "snobs," and "cute but flat-chested."

He was nervous, too. What if the girls thought he was a dork? What if he couldn't think of anything to say to them? What if he didn't know the same dances they did?

Were the other guys nervous? he wondered. They didn't show it, though the night of the dance everyone seemed to be taking his time getting ready. David stood in front of the bathroom mirror, carefully combing his hair, which he'd recently had cut in the same short style as the other boys. Chesty and Magoo were still in the showers. McGivern, wearing only a towel wrapped around his waist, was very methodically shaving at the next sink. Dillon, who reeked of cologne, sidled over and peered into the sink, which was filled with sudsy water.

"There's nothing there," he announced to the bathroom full of boys.

"Screw you, Dillon," said McGivern, and he took another swipe at his face with the razor.

"Connors!" Dillon summoned his friend to back him up. "Do you see any trace of whisker in this bowl?"

"Screw you, guys. I shave twice a week."

Connors bent over, pressed his face close to the edge of the sink, and stuck his finger in the water. "Wait a minute," he said. "I think I got one."

He held his finger up to the light and examined it more closely. "No. It's snot," he concluded, wiping his hand against Van Kelt's arm.

"What a keen sense of humor," Van Kelt said in his deadpan manner.

McGivern paid them no attention. His mind was already on the evening ahead. "If I don't get total tit tonight, I'll be using this razor to cut my throat," he moaned. "As I see it, sex is my only reason for living."

"Then be careful you don't cut your hand," Dillon snickered.

David thought the guys were being too hard on McGivern. "Life isn't over yet, Mac," he said, trying to console him. "You can't tell from one interview."

McGivern splashed cold water on his face and patted it with a washcloth. "Oh? When the guy from Princeton says they *might* be willing to accept a C in French, and you're flunking French, life is pretty much over. Don't you agree?"

"Princeton isn't the only school in the Ivy League," David reminded him.

"Would someone please explain this to our friend from Scranton?" McGivern appealed to the rest of the boys.

"He *has* to go to Princeton. Five generations of McGiverns have gone to Princeton," Reece said matter-of-factly.

"If I don't get in, it means the blood has gone thin. It means the others all had cocks, but I just have a wee-wee." McGivern clutched at his groin to illustrate his point.

"Excuse me if I have a hard time sympathizing," said Dillon, reaching for his mouthwash. "Harvard wants monthly reports on me."

"How about you, Greene?" asked Van Kelt.

"Touch and go. I'm pulling a C in French. C plus, maybe."

Connor pressed two fingers alongside the pimple

in the middle of his forehead. "Don't sweat it," he said, staring into the mirror. "Dillon's brother graduates this year, and the backup Harvard quarterbacks are all thumbs. You're in."

"I wouldn't go to Harvard if you paid me," sneered Chesty, who had finally emerged from the shower and was vigorously toweling himself dry. "All those Jews and communists."

A shiver shook David's body. He blinked, took a breath, and glanced cautiously from Dillon to Reece and Van Kelt. They couldn't all agree with Chesty. They were too smart. They had to know better.

Van Kelt spit out a mouthful of water and turned to face Chesty. "And that's just the faculty," he said.

The palms of David's hands were wet with sweat as he folded his arms across his chest.

"You're both so full of shit," said Dillon.

Finally, David thought, and he waited for Dillon to tear into Chesty and Van Kelt.

Magoo had been quietly brushing his hair. Now he squinted through the steam that covered his glasses and said, "Jew lover."

"What do I care how many Jews are at Harvard?" Dillon shrugged. "They're not in the clubs. You don't have to room with them. It's just like Princeton. You don't have to be around them if you don't want to."

"Why would you want to?" Van Kelt's question hovered between genuine curiosity and disdain.

"I *don't* want to!" Dillon angrily defended himself.

"Then don't go to Harvard," Van Kelt said, defying Dillon to crack his logic.

Dillon shook his head in frustration. "Help," he said.

David's heart was pounding so loudly he was surprised that no one else could hear it. He felt frightened—although he didn't know of whom or what. His mouth was dry, and he had to swallow hard to get rid of the lump in his throat before he could speak. "How would you ever know?" he asked.

"What?"

"If you were with . . . them."

"Are you kidding? How would you *not* know? It's kinda hard to miss a hebe." Dillon took one last look in the mirror and was apparently satisfied with what he found there. "Girls, eat your hearts out." He grinned.

He danced out of the bathroom with his hands high above his head like a winning prizefighter. One by one the rest of the group slowly drifted after him until David was left alone to wonder what his grandfather would have done in his place.

Would Grandpa have thrown up his fists and educated Dillon with a swift poke in the nose? What would that have accomplished, other than proving that "hebes" knew how to fight, too?

He contemplated his reflection in the mirror and tried to discover the parts of him that revealed his Jewishness. Perhaps his father was right. He didn't owe anyone any explanations. He wanted to fit in, and he had succeeded wonderfully well up until now. And in the end he would have the last laugh, because Dillon, Van Kelt, and the rest would never know—unless he chose to tell them—that a dreaded Jew was moving among them.

The Overbrook School was located in the next town over, just seven miles from the St. Matthew's campus. But except for those rare occasions when students of the two schools were allowed to socialize at a dance or a football game, the Overbrook girls were as far away and out of reach as a distant planet in another solar system.

Many of the students had been friends for years, as had their parents and grandparents before them. But away from home, thrown together at a school dance with the girls dressed up in pearls and high heels and the boys in their best sports jackets, some mysterious force of nature took over. The boys inevitably metamorphosed into awkward, tongue-tied creatures who treated the girls like creatures from another universe.

The girls worked hard to get the boys to feel at ease. They dimmed the lights in the field house, normally reserved for floor hockey games and modern dance classes, and festooned it with colored streamers and balloons. They hired a band of five pre-med students from Amherst to play the latest hits. They prepared hundreds of dainty, crustless tea sandwiches, baked brownies and chocolate chip cookies, and concocted a fizzy fruit punch out of ginger ale and cranberry juice.

Nevertheless, all except the bravest boys spent the early part of the evening telling dirty jokes in the corner or gorging themselves on refreshments.

Girls were so *different*. They played field hockey instead of football and giggled over their losses. They talked endlessly about Doris Day and Rock Hudson, about mummy and daddy, about going to Bermuda for Easter break. They blushed at even the faintest hint of vulgarity. They smelled of delicate spring flowers.

Just as inevitably, midway through the evening the moment arrived when the fragrance of their mingled perfumes lured the boys out of the corners and onto the dance floor. The band began playing the slow, romantic tunes. Some of the couples were dancing close enough that the chaperons had to tap them on the shoulder and smilingly utter that oldest of prep school chaperon lines, "Don't forget to make room for the Holy Ghost."

David stood alone, observing the scene. He hadn't yet mustered the courage to venture onto the dance floor, but he felt a definite sense of superiority. Whatever advantages his friends might have over him, they sure didn't know how to jitterbug. Why weren't they snapping their fingers, shaking their hips, and moving their feet? Hadn't these guys ever watched "American Bandstand"?

Then the band turned down the volume and segued into the chorus of "Earth Angel." The mood shifted, and David suddenly spotted the girl of his dreams. She was better than an earth angel. She was a goddess. And she was dancing with Dillon.

Reece came over to join him. "You can roll your tongue back up," he said, following David's moon-struck gaze.

"God, she's beautiful," David said reverentially.

Reece nodded. "Sally Wheeler. Dillon says she's his girlfriend."

"Is she?" David steeled himself for Reece's response.

It came swiftly and cruelly. "I guess so. That's the word."

Unmindful of the wound he'd inflicted on his friend, Reece departed to get another brownie while David stood staring at the girl in Dillon's arms.

She looked like a movie star. In fact, it would not have been exaggerating to say she looked a lot like Marilyn Monroe. She was even dressed like Marilyn Monroe in a short-sleeved, fuzzy pink sweater that showed off her not-insignificant breasts to stunning advantage. She had wavy blond hair that fell to just below her shoulders and huge blue eyes that became even huger every time she laughed at one of Dillon's jokes.

Sally Wheeler. She even had a movie star's name.

He couldn't tear his eyes away from her. She had exquisitely pale skin that was marred by not a single pimple or blemish. Her figure was as well-proportioned as any pinup girl's. She smiled easily and often. Her lips, defined with blood-red lipstick, cried out to be kissed. David ached to answer the summons.

It was just his bad luck that she and Dillon appeared to be as cozy a twosome as peanut butter and jelly.

Silently cursing his wretched luck, David decided he couldn't stand by idly while his heart broke from the pain of unrequited love. He straightened his tie, ran his fingers through his hair, and moved across the floor to find a partner. At the very least he could give his friends a lesson in how rock 'n' roll was meant to be danced.

His ultracool, Philadelphia–style moves quickly made him the center of attention. Dillon and Sally Wheeler were among the group that crowded around for a closer look. "Isn't that your new quarterback?" asked Sally.

"Yeah. David Greene. Guy must be half nigger," Dillon said admiringly. "He can really dance."

The song ended, and David pulled a two-handed, over-the-head turn on his breathless partner.

"Introduce me," said Sally. She slipped her arm through Dillon's and led him over to David.

"Hey, you move as good on the floor as you do on the field," said Dillon. "Sally Wheeler, David Greene."

Sally smiled, and David discovered a dimple in her left cheek. "Hello," she said.

"Hi." He stuck out his hand, then immediately wanted to kick himself for coming across so square. But Sally didn't seem to mind. Her fingers and palm were warm and soft to the touch. David wished Dillon would disappear so he could be alone with her.

"Dillon!" Van Kelt, gesturing to his pal from across the room, provided an answer to David's prayer. "C'mere a minute."

"Be back in a minute," said Dillon.

"No rush," Sally told him with a sweet smile.

She was a goddess, no question about it. David

searched desperately for something to say. "I saw you dancing . . ." His voice trailed off. He couldn't think how to finish the sentence.

"Yes . . ." Her perfect hand, encircled by a thick gold bracelet, fiddled with the string of pearls that hung around her perfect neck.

". . . with Dillon," he concluded, hating himself for sounding like a complete jerk.

"I saw you, too," said Sally, still playing with her pearls.

"Dillon's a great guy."

She shrugged and looked across the floor. "He's fun."

"Yeah." He was sure that she hated him. At the very least, she was bored by him. He tried desperately to think of something clever to recapture her interest, but it was hopeless. His mind had gone numb from the strain of standing so close to her. He wanted to bury his face in her golden hair. Touch her cheeks. Hold her hand forever.

"You think he'll go to Harvard?" he said lamely.

"Is that what you do with your spare time?"

"What?"

She fixed her eyes on his and dared him to look away. Then she smiled. "Worry about Dillon?"

He got the message. "I don't have any spare time," he said, returning the smile.

"Great song, huh?"

The band was playing "Sincerely," one of his favorites.

"Uh-huh," he said.

Sally stood with one hand on her hip, tapping her

foot to the beat of the music. Finally it dawned on him. "Would you like to dance?" he asked.

She said nothing, just drifted into his arms and rested her cheek on his shoulder. She was an excellent dancer—graceful and light on her feet—and she followed him easily.

For a few minutes he was content to put his arm around her and feel her body curving against his. But the pleasure was too intense, and there was something he needed to know.

"Are you two going steady?" he asked, trying to keep his voice steady.

Sally tilted her head slightly backwards and widened her eyes. "Our families share some woods in Maine. We've known each other since we were five. We're thrown together so often some people think we're going steady. But some people think wrong."

He wanted to shout with relief. Instead he managed a joke. "Yeah, I know how it is. My family shares some woods in Pennsylvania." He twirled her around the floor, then delivered the punch line. "Only we share them with three thousand other people."

Sally giggled. "You must think I'm a spoiled brat, and I am," she admitted, sounding as if she cared what he thought of her.

He closed his eyes and inhaled the scent of lilacs in her hair. "I think you're so . . . pretty."

His boldness surprised them both. Sally stopped in midstep. He could feel his cheeks flushing with embarrassment. "I sound like a real nosebleed," he said. "Don't tell your roommate, okay?"

"You know my roommate?" She sounded surprised, and slightly bothered, by the possibility.

"No, I just don't want her to know."

Sally wrinkled up her nose and leaned closer, as if she were about to tell him the most wonderful secret. "I think," she said, lowering her voice, "you're pretty, too."

He was still trying to come up with an adequate response when Dillon tapped him on the shoulder. "Thanks for taking care of my girl," Dillon said, waltzing Sally out of David's grasp. "Try the punch."

Was it his imagination, or had Sally winked at him behind Dillon's back as he danced across the floor? Shit. He didn't give a damn about the punch, which Dillon and Van Kelt must have spiked. So much for Van Kelt passing himself off as the holier-than-thou prefect. And so much for Dillon calling Sally his girl.

She had all but spelled out her availability. Now it was up to him to figure out a way to go after her.

The Columbus Day weekend was the boys' last break before midterms commenced the following Monday. David was so immersed in cramming for his first set of prep school exams that he had hardly a free moment to brood over Sally Wheeler. His only consolation came from knowing that the other boys felt just as overwhelmed.

The consensus was that Mr. Cleary deserved the booby prize for most hideously unfair midterm exercise. He had assigned each of the boys a poem out of English literature, which they were to trans-

late into idiomatic French and recite aloud in class.
It was a double-barreled attack. They not only had
to work their asses off to get the translation right
and memorize the damn poem, but they also had to
make fools of themselves in public by stumbling
through the recitation.

Even Reece, who had lived in Paris for a year and
spoke the language with a decent accent, agreed
that Mr. Cleary had stepped over the line. The
assignment verged on cruel and unusual punishment, a denial of their constitutional rights as
Americans. Unfortunately, there wasn't a damn
thing they could do about it except sweat over the
translations and pray.

The morning of the midterm McGivern, the
recognized dunce of the class, was still practicing
his translation of Keats's poem about the Elgin
Marbles as the boys made their way to Mr. Cleary's
classroom.

*"Mon esprit n'est pas assez fort. . . . La mortalité
presse lourdement sur moi comme un sommeil sans
le vouloir,"* he proclaimed, with about as much
animation as a condemned man on his way to the
gallows.

"Now *that's* French!" said David, hoping to
bolster McGivern's spirits.

"It better be," McGivern said grimly. "It's worth
ten percent of the final."

"If Brigitte Bardot was here and heard that
French, she'd take off all her clothes," Connors
chimed in.

"I don't think she *has* any clothes," guffawed
Dillon.

"This is true," said Van Kelt, sounding wistful. "Only panties. Drawers and drawers of panties."

The boys moaned in unison and silently abandoned themselves to reveries of Bardot's bikini underwear. But their visions of skimpy silk panties were shattered by reality as soon as they walked into class. Mr. Cleary was waiting and ready to pounce. His grade book and pen at the ready, he seated himself at the back of the room, and he sent the boys up to his desk one by one to deliver their translations.

McGivern was the fourth to be called on. He staggered up to the front of the room, shot his friends a look of helpless desperation, and began in a low, tremulous voice:

"En voyant les Marbres d'Elgin. Mon esprit n'est pas assez fort . . . Mon esprit est trop faible. La mortalité presse lourdement sur moi comme un sommeil sans le vouloir . . ."

"Monsieur McGivern, *pas 'sans le vouloir.'"* Mr. Cleary interrupted him to correct his translation. *"Ce n'est pas grammatiquement correct. 'Involontaire—un sommeil involontaire.'"*

Beads of sweat dripped from McGivern's forehead and top lip. He swiped them away with his jacket sleeve and struggled to grasp Mr. Cleary's comment. Okay, his grammar was off. He had used the wrong word for "involuntary." Not so bad. Even Cleary couldn't justify failing him for one mistake.

". . . comme un sommeil involontaire," he went on, correcting his error. *"Et chaque sommet imaginaire it raide de la difficulté de Dieu . . ."*

"Pas 'de Dieu,' Monsieur McGivern, *'divine.' 'De la difficulté divine.'"* Mr. Cleary broke in again to criticize his choice of words.

McGivern chewed on his lower lip and nodded mechanically. The next section of the poem always gave him the most trouble. If he could make it through the next couple of lines without folding, he would probably be all right.

"De la difficulté divine me dit que je dois mourir comme un aigle malade qui regard le ciel," he said, stumbling over the image of the dying eagle staring up at the sky. The eagle was sick *and* dying . . . which was just how he felt right now. He cracked his knuckles and continued. *"Cependant c'est une douce luxe . . ."*

"Repetez, douce luxe." Mr. Cleary pursed his lips to illustrate the proper position of the mouth and tongue. His tone, as he demanded that McGivern repeat the last phrase, dripped contempt.

"Douce luxe?" McGivern said hopefully.

The teacher buried his head in his hands. *"Encore."* He needed to hear it again and again, until McGivern properly pronounced the words.

"Douce luxe."

Mr. Cleary sighed. *"Continuez."*

". . . c'est une douce luxe de crier . . ." McGivern's delivery was tentative and faltering. He felt, with each additional correction, as if Mr. Cleary were pounding him over the head with a paddle.

"Monsieur McGivern, *crier, c'est ce qu'on fait quand on a très peur!"* Mr. Cleary shouted, determined to teach his students the difference between "to cry out in fear" and "to cry." *"Pleurer! Pleurer! Pleurer!"*

Pleurer, the French word for the verb "to cry," echoed through the hushed classroom. The boys sat still as the dead. No one moved. No one even twitched a muscle.

For one crazy moment McGivern thought Mr. Cleary was commanding him to cry. Then, to his horror, he felt himself about to burst into tears. Broken and shamed, he glanced slack-mouthed at his pals, then bolted for the door.

"Au revoir, Monsieur McGivern," Mr. Cleary called after him. The door slammed shut. McGivern disappeared from sight.

Mr. Cleary chuckled and turned back to his students. He was ready and eager for his next victim.

"That asshole Cleary!" Dillon exploded.

The bell had rung, class had been dismissed, and the boys were out in the hall, venting their fury.

"Sadistic shit-eater!" raged Connors.

"God, Mac was doing all right," said Reece, shaken by McGivern's humiliation.

"What about Mac?" David asked. "Is he gonna be okay?"

"Yeah, just leave him alone for a while," said Connors, who'd roomed with McGivern since ninth grade.

"Poor guy," Van Kelt said sympathetically. "He really took it."

The other boys nodded. Van Kelt had summed up their feelings. But for the rest of the day David couldn't stop thinking about McGivern. He couldn't get out of his mind the memory of McGivern cracking his knuckles and wiping the sweat from his brow as Mr. Cleary stomped all over his pride.

7

Greene! Phone! It's your sister!"

David pulled his head out of his chemistry text. His sister? Why was Sarah calling him? He glanced at his watch and saw that it was almost eleven o'clock. Why so late? Was something wrong at home? Had something happened to Petey or Pop?

He jumped off his bed, hurried down the hall, and grabbed the telephone receiver. "Hello? Sarah, what's up?"

"I didn't even know you had a sister," said the girl's voice at the other end.

"Who is this?" he asked, daring to hope it was the girl he most wanted to hear from.

"It's Sally Wheeler."

He thought, Thank you, God. Aloud, trying to sound cool and casual, he said, "Hi. Where are you?"

"I'm at school," said Sally with a breathy giggle. "In the dorm."

Mr. Cleary appeared at the end of the corridor. He looked at David, tapped his watch, and held up both hands. Ten minutes to curfew. David nodded. The man was evil. He deserved to be exiled to a deserted island like that other French–speaking tyrant, Napoleon Bonaparte.

"Are you studying?" asked Sally.

"Yeah," David said, remembering the sensation of her breasts pressed against his chest. "Chemistry."

"I hate chemistry."

"Me, too," said David, though in fact it was one of his favorite subjects.

There was a long pause. Then Sally said, "You ever go to Skip's Diner?"

He was about to tell her he'd never even heard of the place when Connors walked past, stopped, and whispered, "Have you seen McGivern?"

"Hold on a sec," David told Sally. He covered the receiver with his hand and shook his head. "No, haven't you?" he asked Connors.

"Not since French class. It's almost lights out. Where the hell is he?"

"Check with Dillon and Van Kelt," David suggested.

Connors frowned. He hadn't seen McGivern since French class. Mac was crazy, but he'd never pulled a disappearing act. "Yeah, okay," he muttered, and he continued down the hall to Dillon's room.

"I'm back," said David into the phone. "Skip's Diner?"

"It's in town, kind of a hangout," Sally explained. "I thought tomorrow night, if you weren't busy with chemistry, we could . . . we could go." She giggled softly. "God, my mother would throw a fit."

"Your mother? Why?" David asked.

More giggling. Then, "Here I am, calling up a boy for a date. Shameful."

David didn't care what her mother might think. Sally was incredible. The most wonderful, beautiful, gutsy girl in the world. "What time?" he said, wondering how he could get Mr. Cleary to excuse him from study hall. That, however, was a small detail. He would be there tomorrow night at Skip's Diner. He would have walked to the North Pole if that's where Sally Wheeler had wanted to meet him.

Ten minutes later David was back in his room with Reece, getting ready to go to sleep. Mr. Cleary had just rung the lights-out bell when Connors stuck his head in the room and said, "He still hasn't shown up."

He didn't need to say another word. McGivern was about to get himself into serious trouble. They had to find him and stop him before it was too late.

Mac was shaving. He had no idea why he was shaving. He only knew that it felt like the right thing to do. His suitcase, into which he had hastily stuffed as many of his possessions as would fit, lay open on the floor next to his sink. He glanced down and noticed that he hadn't done a very good job of packing. So what, he decided. Neatness didn't count anymore.

He wasn't doing a very good job of shaving, either. His hand was shaking so badly that every time he drew the razor across his cheek or chin, threads of blood erupted from yet another jagged cut.

Luckily, he was alone in the bathroom. He had deliberately waited until just before lights out to sneak out of the maids' pantry where he'd hidden for the last couple of hours. He was the Shadow, making his way through the darkness of the night to wreak vengeance upon his enemies and persecutors.

If only his hand would stop shaking.

His blazer lay balled up on top of his suitcase. He pulled it on and adjusted his school tie in the mirror. He had orders to wear a disguise when he conducted this most dangerous mission.

If only he wasn't so cold. If only he could stop trembling.

He wiped the bloodied razor against his pants and stuck it into his pocket. His face, from his forehead to his chin, was streaked with blood. Ugh. All those globs of blood made his stomach go queasy.

He went into one of the stalls, grabbed a handful of toilet paper, and covered his face with ragged bits of the paper to stop the bleeding. He looked like shit, but what the hell did he care? He was on a mission. He was the Shadow. He was invisible.

The air felt damp and cold against David's face as he skirted the woods that edged the campus, calling McGivern's name as loudly as he dared. He switched on his flashlight and directed the beam along the dirt paths and into the thickets of bushes. Another beam shining across an open field answered his. Connors, Reece, Van Kelt, Dillon . . . they were all out there, combing the dark for McGivern.

The night felt dangerous. Behind every building and tree lurked infinite possibilities out of David's worst nightmares. What if they didn't find McGivern? Or worse, what if they found McGivern too late to help him?

A scene from a World War II movie played in David's head. Captured Allied officers were searching for one of their friends who was foolishly trying to break out of a Nazi prisoner-of-war camp. He was in terrible danger. The commandant had learned that someone might try to escape. The guards had been alerted. The dogs were straining at their leashes. The Allies had to find him before he fled under the barbed wire and into the waiting arms of the Nazis.

Stop it! David told himself. He zipped up his jacket against the damp, cold wind. He was in Massachusetts, not Nazi Germany. There were no dogs prowling the campus, tracking their prey. Even if McGivern got caught somewhere he wasn't supposed to be, Dr. Bartram wasn't about to shoot him at dawn.

Earlier in the week workmen had dug a trench behind one of the dorms to repair a burst pipe. They had barricaded the site with sawhorses to warn people away from the open pit. Now, coming up on the sawhorses, David saw a gleam of light.

"Connors?" he whispered.

"Jesus!" Startled, Connors stepped out of the darkness. "You find him?"

"No, we're gonna check the lake."

This was Van Kelt's idea. David wasn't exactly sure *why* they were checking the lake, except that was what people in the movies and on TV always did when someone was missing.

The other boys were already gathered along the bank of the lake, which was just deep enough for the crew team to practice its strokes. Van Kelt and Dillon volunteered to search the boat house, while Connors trudged back and forth along the shore, aiming his flashlight beneath the murky surface of the water.

Reece and David circled the boat house, looking for footprints or any other clues that might lead them to Mac. A narrow shed protruded from the side of the building closest to the lake. It was doubtful that even someone as short and thin as McGivern could fit inside so shallow a space, but Reece nevertheless pushed aside the metal bolt and opened the door. David shone his flashlight inside. Just as they'd thought. Nothing but rows of neatly stacked oars.

The boys gave up on the lake idea and adjourned to the steps of one of the academic buildings to plot their next move.

"I think we have to tell somebody," said Van Kelt, tossing his flashlight from one hand to the other.

"Maybe he went off and got drunk," said David.

Connors shook his head. "Mac never drinks. Hates the taste."

"Do you think he went home?" Dillon asked.

Back in the dorm David had asked Connors the same question. Maybe McGivern had walked into town and caught a bus to New York. But Connors had rejected that scenario. Mac's mother was visiting friends in the south of France, his father was drying out somewhere upstate, and his grandparents had gone to Palm Beach for the season. He had no home to go back to. The family's Park Avenue apartment was locked shut.

Magoo, who was too worried to sit and do nothing, restlessly paced the steps, directing the gleam of his flashlight back and forth along the facade of the building.

Chesty slapped his arms against his body to ward off the cold. "He would have said something," he muttered.

"Isn't that . . . French class?" Magoo said suddenly. He shone his light on an open window three stories up.

The boys followed the path of his beam and saw he was right. Thinking the worst, they flashed their lights on the patch of ground directly below the

125

window. A communal sigh of relief: There was no broken body or brains splattered in the grass. Magoo giggled nervously. For a moment there he'd really been scared.

"Shhh," said Reece, holding up a warning finger. "Don't move. Listen."

The boys froze. In the stillness they could just about make out a barely perceptible murmur, like the sound of a radio filtered through a thick wall. The voice was too far away to be identified. Nor could they hear the words, which were being uttered in a dull monotone. But they all had the same idea at once.

They dashed into the building and stormed up the stairs to the third floor. The door to the French room was partly open. Reece flicked on the light, and the boys crowded inside.

A suitcase lay on top of Mr. Cleary's desk. They heard McGivern before they saw him. A flattened-out version of Mac's normal voice was reciting the poem he had tried to recite earlier that day.

Connors found him hunched on the floor behind Mr. Cleary's desk, swaying gently as he gazed at some distant point in space. His face was dotted with bloodied pieces of toilet paper.

"Mac? Oh, no . . ." Connors broke off as he spotted the message McGivern had written on the blackboard.

Monsieur Cleary *est un merd.*

Mr. Cleary is a murderer.

McGivern's lips contorted in a grotesque imitation of his smile.

David bent over and tried to help him up. "It's all right, Mac. You did fine," he said softly. The boys stood gaping at their friend. "Get some help," he told them.

Van Kelt turned and ran. Connors was crying as he crouched next to his roommate, who didn't respond to either boy's attempts to comfort him.

He resumed the recitation. *"Mon esprit n'est pas assez fort. Mon esprit est trop faible. La mortalité presse lourdement sur moi comme un sommeil involontaire."*

McGivern had finally gotten it right. David listened to him drone on in French and thought about how grotesquely fitting the words were for Mac's state of mind: "My spirit is not strong enough. My spirit is too weak. Mortality presses heavily on me like an unwanted sleep. . . ."

David bit his lip to keep from crying himself. He knelt by Mac's side and solemnly began to recite along with him:

". . . comme un sommeil involontaire. Et chaque sommet imaginaire it raide de la difficulté divine me dit que je dois mourir. Comme un aigle malade qui regard le ciel. Cependant c'est une douce luxe . . ."

He stayed with McGivern until two ambulance attendants showed up. Mac was shivering uncontrollably, and his teeth were chattering like castanets, but his eyes remained fixed in a blank stare. The attendants wrapped him in a blanket to protect him from the chill. Then, propped up by them on either side, he shuffled out of the room with the

127

slow, aimless gait of an old man who has nowhere to go and no reason to get there.

David was about to leave with them when he realized there was something he had forgotten to set right. He walked up to the blackboard, which was still covered with McGivern's message. He picked up a piece of chalk and added an *e* at the end of *merd* to correct the spelling. Then he turned off the lights and followed them down the stairs.

The ambulance was parked on the lawn in front of the chapel. The shriek of its siren, now silent, had alerted the students that something was up. They streamed out of the dorms in their bathrobes and gathered on the green, where the whirling lights from the ambulance illuminated the fear in their eyes.

As the attendants walked past carrying McGivern on a stretcher Dr. Bartram and Mr. Pierce spoke quietly to the knots of boys milling around the ambulance, trying to calm their concerns and get them to go back inside. The chaplain leaned over and whispered a few words in McGivern's ear. But the attendants had given him a sedative. Mac was beyond reach.

His friends stood apart, stunned into silence by what they had seen. Coach McDevitt came hurrying over, and he, too, tried to allay their worries about Mac. Don't worry, he said. He'll be fine. He just needs to relax for a while, get some rest.

David didn't believe him. Mac had looked so beaten and crushed, as if his soul had been turned inside out and stripped of its spirit. Nobody deserved to be destroyed like that. He hated Mr. Cleary for what he done to Mac. When he saw the teacher standing at the back of the crowd, he knew he had to tell him how he felt.

He elbowed his way past the coach and the other onlookers until he stood toe-to-toe with the French teacher. "You did this!" he yelled, giving vent to the terror that had coiled itself around his heart. "You rode him till he broke. You wouldn't let up. You picked on him and picked on him. What did he ever do to you?"

He was one beat away from jumping the startled teacher to show him how justice was meted out in Scranton. But Dillon quickly intervened to save David from his own anger. He grabbed David's arms and hustled him away before he could make good on his unspoken threat of reprisal. Mr. Cleary stared defiantly at the rest of the group, as if daring them to pick up where David had left off. They angrily returned his gaze, but nobody made a move. They all knew better.

Then the ambulance doors closed, the siren wailed, and McGivern was gone.

Whenever Dillon needed a quiet place to think and be alone he would slip over to the boating dock. During the day the area was heavily trafficked by the members of the rowing teams. But after dark it belonged to Dillon. There he would try to find the face of his future in the water lapping against the back of the boat house.

He had brought David there to cool off. The two

of them sat at the edge of the dock, their legs dangling over the side, talking about what had happened to Mac.

"God, did you see him? He didn't even look like himself. He looked like some trapped animal," said David.

"I know it was horrible." The tip of Dillon's cigarette glowed in the darkness. "But David, you can't go after a teacher like that. It's the end if you do."

David felt both justified and ashamed of the way he'd exploded at Mr. Cleary. But for the moment he ignored Dillon's reproof. He was still trying to make sense of Mac's reaction.

"If I told my friends back home about this, they wouldn't believe me," he muttered. "Over a failing grade in French?"

"Good grades. The right school. The right college. The right connections. Those are the keys to the kingdom." Dillon enumerated the tenets of the faith in which he and his friends had been raised. "None of us ever goes off and lives by his wits. We do the things they tell us to do, and then they give us the good life. I goddamn hope we'll like it when we get it."

"What'll happen to Mac?"

"He won't be back," Dillon said flatly.

Did Dillon really feel as detached as he sounded? David peered at him through the murk. But he might as well have been wearing a mask. His expression was impenetrable. "Man, I heard about nervous breakdowns, but I always thought they happened to women, you know, who were forty years old. I never realized a kid my age could have one."

"When I was a sophomore," said Dillon, "there was this senior, Mark Bozman. He killed himself. Hanged himself in the gym."

He tossed what was left of his cigarette into the water. It landed with a hiss and bobbed out of sight.

David pictured some kid his age hanging from a beam in the gym. "Why?" he asked, almost physically sickened by the image.

"He . . . uh . . . he didn't get into Harvard." Dillon laughed weakly at the absurdity of his answer.

"Shit!" said David. He leaned back on his elbows and stared up at the star-filled sky. "I want to go to Harvard, but I'll be goddamned if I croak myself if I don't."

They fell silent and lost themselves in the hush of the night, disturbed only by the muffled slap of the water as it hit the overturned boats tied up next to the dock.

"I envy you," Dillon said after a few minutes. He struck a match and cupped his hands around the flickering flame to light another cigarette.

"Me? Why?"

"If you get what you want, you'll deserve it. If you don't, you'll manage. You don't have to live up to anybody else's expectations. You are who you are. That's what really draws people to you—not that you're the cool quarterback."

The dampness from the wooden planks was

seeping into David's bones. He pushed himself up to his feet, took a walk down to the end of the dock, and pondered Dillon's view of him. Yes, it was true that he wasn't weighed down with the burden of a famous older brother, or a family heritage that decreed he was a failure if he didn't get into a particular university.

Sure, he'd survive even if he didn't get accepted at Harvard or Princeton or Yale. An Ivy League degree wasn't all that important to him. He could have a perfectly good existence without a fancy diploma.

But what about Pop's expectations of him? Wasn't he, at least to some degree, living the life Pop would have wanted for himself? And wasn't there always some part of him second-guessing who he was supposed to be?

Still, if he had to choose, he would much rather stick with his family's history than Dillon's. That thought made him feel guilty, so he said, "Come on, you're the most popular guy on campus."

"If my name wasn't Dillon, it'd be different."

"Bullshit."

"Don't forget my last name is Dillon. Son of Grayson Junior, brother of Grayson the Third. I'm a Dillon. I'm part of those right connections I was telling you about." Dillon made a noise in his throat that was intended to be a laugh but came out sounding more like whimper. He stood up and headed back to the boat house.

"People don't care about that," said David, following him down the dock.

As usual, Dillon had to have the last word. "You'll see."

The boys were up past midnight, whispering and scheming about how to repay Mr. Cleary for what he had done to McGivern. Connors thought they should pool their money and buy him a subscription to *Playboy*. Dr. Bartram would have a fit—probably even fire Mr. Cleary—as soon as he found out that a copy of the magazine was being delivered to the dorm every month.

"But what if Dr. Bartram *doesn't* find out?" asked the ever-practical Van Kelt. "Then we're the idiots for wasting our hard-earned allowances, *and* Mr. Cleary gets to look at the pictures!"

Magoo's suggestion that they sneak into his room and steal his favorite Princeton sweater got a round of applause until Reece pointed out that Mr. Cleary might think it had gone missing in the laundry and order another one.

"Psychological warfare," said David. "Hit him where it hurts him the most."

"His car!" the boys chorused.

"He and that MG are a real steady item. I bet he's just sorry he can't sleep with her," Chesty guffawed.

"We can't steal a car," Reece pointed out. "First we'd have to steal the keys, and he probably keeps them hanging from a chain around his neck, close to his heart."

"Forget it," Dillon said pessimistically. "There's just no way."

But David couldn't get out of his mind the memory of McGivern's face. The next morning, as the sun was rising and he jogged his two miles around the campus, he couldn't stop staring at Mr. Cleary's car, parked on the roadway.

The solution came to him that same afternoon during football practice. The sky was a slate November gray. The air smelled like snow. Coach had them in serious training for the upcoming all-important game against St. Luke's. Dressed in their full uniforms, they were doing double- and triple-time laps around the field.

David suddenly stopped dead in his tracks. "There is a way!" he declared, and he summoned his friends into a huddle.

Upon review, the consensus was that his idea was nothing short of brilliant.

The sentries had been posted—one in the window overlooking the quad, two at either end of the road that abutted the parking lot. At seven-thirty P.M. sharp, just when Mr. Cleary was setting out as usual for his evening constitutional, the big shots of the football team were gathered around his MG, preparing to implement David's plan.

The boys squatted low to the ground, firmly gripped the rear of the car, and waited for the quarterback to call the signals.

"One, two, three!" David barked.

Grunting and heaving, they picked up the back of the MG and walked it away on its front tires.

Precisely fifteen minutes later Mr. Cleary was coming into the home stretch of his route. The sentry standing watch in the window saw him coming. He signaled the information via flashlight to one of his friends who stood waiting in the shadows a few feet from the dorm.

The boy, who had on a plaid tam and matching scarf similar to the ones Mr. Cleary always wore, stepped out onto the road. "Evening, sir," he greeted him.

"Evening," said Mr. Cleary.

A few feet further down the road he passed a second student, who was likewise dressed in a tam and scarf. Oddly, the boy was also brandishing a carved wooden walking stick, much like the one that Mr. Cleary carried on his evening walks.

"Evening, sir," said the boy.

"What the—" Mr. Cleary muttered, glancing back at the boy. Coincidence, he decided. Merely coincidence.

"Evening, sir." A third boy appeared along the road. He, too, wore a tam and scarf and carried a walking stick in his hand. He gave a cheerful wave, and Mr. Cleary noticed that he was holding a pipe, just like the one he smoked.

Mr. Cleary turned to give the boy a second look and saw him sprinting madly down the road. "What the hell?" he said aloud. This was no mere coincidence. This smacked of insubordination.

The three encounters had rattled him. He was looking forward to getting back and pouring himself his daily snifter of brandy. He hurried into the dorm, then stopped short just outside his room. The most peculiar noises were issuing forth from the other side of his door. It almost sounded as if . . . But no, how could it be? Ridiculous, he told himself. Impossible. Clearly he was imagining things.

Nevertheless, he pushed the door open with no small amount of trepidation. To his horror, there, smack in the middle of the room, sat his precious MG. Its engine chugged contentedly, filling the cramped quarters with noxious toxic fumes.

Outside his room, crowding the stairwells and hanging from the banisters, the boys waited tensely for Mr. Cleary's reaction. It wasn't long in coming. His hysterical, high-pitched screams and violent fits of coughing reverberated all up and down the corridors of Iselin Hall.

David and his friends swung from the overhead pipes like monkeys, hooting and whooping with glee. Victory was theirs! McGivern was avenged!

Because of the Cleary caper, David had had to postpone his date with Sally until the next evening. Contrary to his worst fears, it had been surprisingly easy to sneak off campus and find Skip's Diner.

Sally was already there, waiting for him in a booth at the back of the restaurant. She was studying the menu, her nose wrinkling in concentration as she deliberated over what to order.

When she looked up and waved hello he almost turned and ran. She was so beautiful . . . even more beautiful than he had remembered. When he sat down across from her he noticed that her eyes crinkled when she smiled, and that one front tooth slightly overlapped the other. For some inexplicable reason he found that tiny flaw in her otherwise perfect face deeply exciting.

They both decided on hamburgers, fries, and Coke, though he was sure he wouldn't be able to eat a bite. But by the time the food came an amazing thing had happened. He was talking and laughing with Sally as easily as if she were one of the girls from back home.

When there was nothing left on their plates but smears of ketchup and little scraps of bun, Sally decided she wanted a cigarette. David watched in fascination as she delicately extracted one from the package and held it between her two slender fingers.

He automatically reached for the book of matches and lit the cigarette for her. To his great surprise and pleasure, she took that opportunity to put her hands over his.

"You don't smoke?" she said, delicately exhaling.

"No. I tried it, but it didn't take," said David.

"God, you're too good," she teased. "Is that to impress the mothers?"

"What mothers?"

"Of all your girlfriends."

"No," he replied, trying to keep a straight face. "Too many to try."

Sally smiled, piqued by the challenge. "You were talking about Saturdays in Scranton."

"Oh, yeah." He stirred what was left of his Coke with the straw. "Garbage day. We had to haul our trash to the dump, which is this deep pit three miles out of town."

She made a face, and he wondered whether he had totally screwed up. He could hardly believe he was telling her all this personal stuff from his childhood. But some inner compulsion forced him to continue. "Hey, don't knock it. This one day my father and I see these two guys, and one of them's got a rope around his waist, and he's holding a net bag, and his buddy holds the other end of the rope and lowers him into the pit."

"Yuk! What for?"

"They were scavenging for tin cans."

"God, who'd want to do that?" She leaned forward, as if the answer truly mattered to her, and he loved her even more for that.

"That's what I said to my old man. He gave me a long, hard look and said, 'Davy, it's an honest living.' I never forgot that. He made me go through our garbage and pick out the cans for them."

She was staring at him, tilting her head and widening her eyes as she had the night they'd met at the dance.

"You want another Coke?" he asked, nervous now that he'd told her too much about himself. "Hello? Sally?"

"You're so different . . . from the other boys," she said.

A flicker of apprehension tickled at the back of his neck. "How's that?"

"The other boys, like Dillon, you know everything about them in two minutes. But you . . ."

He laughed with relief. *"Four* minutes, easy."

She dragged on the cigarette, inhaling slowly and

just as slowly releasing the smoke. David felt as if he were melting inside.

"You have a serious side," she said.

He was both thrilled and terrified that she had figured him out so quickly.

The waitress brought him their check. He glanced at his watch and saw that if he didn't leave soon, Sally would miss her bus and he'd never get back to the dorm before lights out. He quickly paid the bill, helped Sally on with her coat, and hurried her outside.

The bus was just pulling up in front of the diner. Should he kiss her good night? he wondered. Naw, not on their first date. She'd think he was too forward.

She squeezed his hand and walked up the steps of the bus. "Night, David," she said.

"Can I call you?" he asked.

"You better." She shook a warning finger at him, smiled, and disappeared inside the bus.

The door slammed shut. A second later it opened again, and Sally came rushing down the steps. She gave him a quick, gentle kiss on the lips, then just as quickly was gone again.

David stood on the sidewalk, immobile as a statue, until long after the bus had vanished from sight. Sally Wheeler had kissed him. On the lips.

Life had never been so sweet.

8

It was the kind of flawless New England mid–November day that seemed to have been specially ordered up for playing football. The weather was sunny, clear, and brisk. The sky was a vast expanse of crystalline blue, marred only by the faintest wisps of cloud floating in the distance. The weatherman was predicting a high of fifty degrees for the afternoon. It was Homecoming Saturday, that annual rite when relatives and alumni converged to watch the boys from St. Matthew's defend their honor against their arch rivals from St. Luke's.

The families had begun arriving right after breakfast. They piled out of their limousines and station wagons with their scarves and blankets, picnic hampers and thermoses. Except for a few other boys whose parents couldn't make it back from Europe or elsewhere, David was the only student unrepresented by any member of his family.

He'd told his friends that of course he wished his father could be there to see the big game. But in fact he was just as glad Pop couldn't take the day off. It was hard to imagine him having a conversation with the other parents. He looked, dressed, even sounded so different from all of them. And what would he talk about—his job at the mine? For Pop, being a foreman was a big deal, but it wouldn't mean diddlysquat to the lawyers, bankers, and doctors whose sons went to school with David.

The custom on Homecoming Day was for the boys to eat lunch and dinner with their families. Dinner reservations were booked months in advance at the best restaurants in the area. But most people ate picnic lunches served off the backs of their station wagons. It was called "tailgating," and the atmosphere felt like one big party, with everyone greeting old friends as they passed around the sandwiches and drinks.

Over at the stadium a preliminary soccer game was in progress, and the stands were already filling up. But a few diehard picnickers still lingered over their lunches in the parking lot. Dillon's family was among them, reminiscing with Sally Wheeler's parents, whom they hadn't seen since they'd closed their homes in Maine after Labor Day.

"We'll finish off our coffee, and then we'll finish off St. Luke's," Grayson Dillon was saying, pouring what was left in the thermos into his cup.

"I'll drink to that. It's about time," said Dillon's older brother Gray.

"Grayson, don't inspire me to increase my bet," chuckled Sally's father. "History has proved it. You can't beat St. Luke's."

"This year is going to be different. You haven't seen our secret weapon," Mr. Dillon said knowingly.

A moment later, as if on cue, Dillon and David came around the corner, already dressed in their football uniforms. Along with the rest of the team, they had eaten their lunch in the dining room under the watchful eye of their coach. His boys weren't about to break training before this, the most important game of the season.

"Hi!" Dillon said, eyeing the cookies and other leftover goodies. "Mom, Dad, Gray, this is David Greene. Mr. and Mrs. Wheeler, David Greene. You met Sally."

"How do you do?" David said, putting on his best manners. "Hello, Sally." He shook hands with the grownups and with Gray, the St. Matthew's legend. He also noticed that it was as difficult for Sally as it was for him to pretend that they'd met just that once at the dance.

What he didn't see was Mrs. Wheeler studying him as carefully as a broody mother hen. If he had, he might have guessed that his name had come up more than once between Sally and her mother.

While Dillon grabbed a handful of cookies and began stuffing them into his mouth, his father turned to David and said, "So, Greene. Are we going to punish St. Luke's for its arrogance?"

"Severely, sir," David replied with a smile.

"Charlie, stop eating," Mrs. Dillon scolded her son. "You'll be playing soon."

"Wheeler here had the misfortune of attending St. Luke's," said Mr. Dillon, gesturing to Sally's father.

"Proud of it." Mr. Wheeler chuckled, and David saw the strong resemblance between father and daughter. "You're at the end of your winning streak, son."

David smiled but tactfully refrained from arguing with him. He was having a hard enough time keeping his eyes off Sally, who was staring at him from beneath lowered lashes.

"You'll join us for dinner?" asked Mrs. Dillon. "No matter who wins."

"Sure, thanks," David said. He nudged Dillon. "We'd better get back."

Dillon grabbed a couple more Fig Newton cookies and threw a kiss at his mother. "Yeah. See you later."

"Nice meeting you," David said politely. He smiled good-bye to Sally, who was standing just behind her mother and brazenly chanced throwing him a kiss.

The girl certainly had nerve, he thought, but he didn't dare reciprocate. Luckily he had an excellent excuse to turn and take off at a run. He and Dillon had a game to win.

"He's very *cute,*" Mrs. Wheeler said quietly to Sally as they began clearing the plates and cups from the tailgate.

Mr. Wheeler, meanwhile, had heard the rumors

about St. Matthew's phenomenal new quarterback and was grilling Dillon's father. "Now, really, Grayson, who found the boy?"

"He applied, just like anybody else." Grayson Dillon shrugged and screwed the top back on the thermos.

His friend looked unconvinced, but Grayson Dillon was too good a courtroom lawyer to give away any secrets. He put on his best poker face and clapped his older son on the back. It was time to go watch St. Matthew's reclaim its glory.

After all the pregame hoopla, after the first formers had marched across the field wearing signs around their necks that read "Lambaste St. Luke's," and St. Luke's had retaliated with their own set of signs that read "Mangle St. Matthew's," after the two teams had been introduced to thunderous applause, the referee stepped into the middle of the field and blew his whistle.

As the visiting team, St. Luke's got first possession of the ball. St. Matthew's kicked off. The game was underway.

David had heard so many stories about the fearsome adversaries from St. Luke's that he was almost disappointed to note they were totally normal high school guys, no bigger or more developed than he and his friends.

But they *were* fierce competitors. Their defensive line mounted a vicious attack on every St. Matthew's pass play. Both quarterbacks were getting sacked hard again and again. Coming into the second quarter the game was dead even, with no touchdowns or field goals on either side.

David succeeded in throwing a series of short passes that moved his team to the thirty-five-yard line. On third down the boys ran in again for the huddle.

Dillon, who had been hit hard by the St. Luke's linebackers, grabbed David's arm before the huddle reformed. "They're looking for a pass," he said. "I'll have the whole right side. I can take it in."

David shook his head. Dillon was a decent halfback, but they needed at least eight yards for a first down, which was a lot to ask of any back.

"C'mon, David, my dad's here," Dillon coaxed.

The boys gathered on the scrimmage line. One of their teammates jogged in from the bench with Coach McDevitt's instructions. "Flood pass to the flats left."

Dillon threw David an openly pleading look that caught David between wanting to follow the coach's orders and feeling bad for Dillon. He hesitated, mentally tossed a coin, and made up his mind. If the play worked, Coach would have nothing to complain about. *If* it worked . . .

"Right formation strong," he called. "Dillon takes it off tackle. Follow Chesty up the hole."

Dillon beamed and punched the air with his hand. They broke the huddle and lined up for the play.

The center snapped the ball to David. Instead of passing to Reece downfield, as Coach had said, David faked a pass and handed it off to Dillon.

Dillon ran no more than three steps to the right before two linemen slipped past the St. Matthew's blockers and creamed him. The ball popped loose from his grasp. A St. Luke's linebacker scooped up the fumbled ball and streaked sixty yards for the touchdown.

The score was seven to zero.

"Get over here!" the coach bellowed to David.

Behind him in the stands, Dillon's father and brother exchanged chagrined looks. But their discomfort was nothing compared to David's. He hung his head and trotted in for the reprimand he knew he deserved.

"I thought we'd catch 'em off guard," he said. The explanation sounded lame even to his ears. There was no good excuse for the play substitution, which both he and the coach were aware might have cost them the game.

"What the hell were you doing?" roared Coach McDevitt, raising his voice another decibel with each new sentence. "I sent in the play. I'm the coach. You're the quarterback. If you don't like the way I run the team, get off!"

Through the rest of the first half David tried to compensate for his earlier screwup by playing the quickest, sharpest game of his career. At eight seconds on the clock the center hiked him the ball. He dropped back, saw the linemen careening toward him, and immediately reversed direction. He slipped low and ran back to the fifty-yard line. Then he unleashed a long, arcing lead pass to Van Kelt, who was racing toward the end zone.

Van Kelt leapt high off the ground. The spinning ball fell into his outstretched hands, bounced, and flew up in the air. He grabbed for it again, but this time the ball slithered through his fingers and onto the turf.

At the end of the first half St. Luke's was still ahead, seven to zero.

The halftime pageantry was in full swing. While the alumni milled about the stands renewing old friendships, marching bands from both schools paraded across the field. Stepping lively, they provided a spirited tempo for the colorfully decorated class floats that slowly circled the outer track of the field.

Behind the floats rolled a fleet of convertibles in which were ensconced the most venerable guests.

The announcer's voice blared over the public address system, introducing each new honoree. As was customary, the oldest graduate brought up the rear of the parade. "Riding in the new black Thunderbird," the announcer declared, "St. Matthew's oldest living alumnus, Franklin Benson, class of 1882."

A wizened old man raised a shaky hand and waved to the crowd. The few wisps of white hair left on his otherwise gleaming scalp ruffled in the breeze as he acknowledged the audience's cheers.

When the stadium finally got quiet again the band tympanist played a shrill drumroll. The members of the St. Matthew's team trotted out to their bench and lined up next to the coach, facing the stands.

"Ladies and gentlemen," the announcer proclaimed, "each year at Homecoming three alumni are named to the St. Matthew's Football Hall of Fame. Until the announcement is made, not even the honorees know who will be named." He paused to heighten the drama, then continued. "This year's inductees to the Hall of Fame are: from the class of '28, U.S. Senator Calvin Knox, fullback . . ."

The audience clapped as the Senator climbed down from the stands to take his place on the field.

"From the class of '43, center, Robert Sanderson . . ."

There was a burst of applause for the second inductee.

"And from the class of '51, the youngest member of the Hall of Fame, quarterback Grayson Dillon the Third."

For a moment Dillon's brother was so overcome with surprise by the unexpected tribute that he froze in his seat. His mother kissed his cheek. His father proudly pumped his hand. Gray finally stood up and ran down the steps.

Gray, a sentimental favorite among the many present who could still recall his brilliant passes, was treated to a rousing ovation as he joined the other two men on the field.

The current St. Matthew's team joined in the cheers of approval. Along with the other boys, Dillon stamped his feet and clapped until his palms were sore. But the smile on his face looked forced. Under cover of the noise in the stadium he leaned closer to David and muttered, "Just what I needed."

The second half began much the same as the first. On every possession both teams were forced sooner or later to punt the ball. Despite strenuous rooting from the stands, neither side was able to gain enough yardage to score. The clock wound down until only three minutes were left to play.

St. Matthew's set up for a field goal on the thirty-five-yard line. David held the ball in place for Connors. Connors squinted through the deepening shadows at the goalposts, took aim, and kicked. The ball went high and straight through the uprights.

The scoreboard registered seven to three.

St. Matthew's quickly regained possession. Their fans shrieked encouragement as David kept hitting short passes to move the ball downfield. He threw a pass to Reece, who tried to break away but was brought down on the ten-yard line.

St. Matthew's converged behind the line of scrimmage to huddle. No one had to tell the boys how badly they needed the win. They'd been practicing for this game all season. Now, with twenty-eight seconds left on the clock and only one more down, it would take close to a miracle to put them ahead.

All of them felt the pressure, but David and Dillon, each for his own reasons, felt it more than the others. "Give me another chance. I can get ten yards, I know I can. Let me make up for that fumble," Dillon begged as they went into the huddle.

But David wasn't about to make the same mistake twice. "The coach calls the plays," he said, angered that Dillon hadn't wised up. Dillon was so intent on proving himself to his father that he was ready to blow whatever slim chance they had to pull this one out.

The boys were waiting for David to call the play. He looked toward the bench to get the coach's signal. The coach nodded his head. David knew what that meant. It was up to David to call the shots.

Fourth down. Twenty-eight seconds.

"What's it gonna be?" asked Dillon.

"We're gonna win this game right now."

A glimmer of hope lit up Dillon's blue eyes.

"Left opposite 110 lead power," said David. "Dillon, I'm coming right behind you. You better block your ass off for me."

Dillon opened his mouth to speak, then just as quickly shut it. Though he couldn't hide his disappointment, he nodded his assent. He'd be there for David every step of the way. He'd block for him like nobody had ever blocked before.

"On one," David said. "Break!"

The huddle broke, and the play resumed. David took the snap and faked right. Connors smashed into the left defensive lineman, and Dillon followed him. David shifted directions and headed toward the hole Connors had created. He grabbed the back of Dillon's shoulder pads and ran downfield with the ball.

"Block where I push you," he shouted to Dillon.

The home team crowd was on its feet as David pushed Dillon directly into the path of the pursuing tacklers. Dillon barreled toward the two hulking defenders and cut them both down with crushing blocks.

David saw the safety speeding at him from the right. He sprinted wildly toward the corner of the end zone. The two boys collided right at the end-zone flag and sent it flying.

Was it a touchdown? Or had David stepped out of bounds inches before the line? The audience collectively held its breath and waited for the official to make his call.

A moment later the official raised his arms above his head to signal a touchdown.

David could hardly hear his own screams above the deafening din from the stands. While Dillon picked himself off the ground, his teammates came running toward the end zone. They swept David up and carried him off the field on their shoulders to the triumphant beat of their fans' applause.

Like many of the other parents, the Dillons and the Wheelers had membership privileges at the nearby Lebanon Country Club, because it was affiliated with their own private clubs in New York and Boston. David had never set foot in so luxurious a place as the club's comfortably spacious dining room, which was all done up in dark wood and stone.

Elegantly uniformed waiters glided unobtrusively among the tables, taking orders, setting down and removing plates, and answering questions with quiet deference. At one end of the room a roaring fire burned in a huge stone fireplace. At the other, three men dressed in tuxedos were playing popular songs on the piano, bass, and saxophone.

Though the room was filled this evening with alumni parents and students from both schools, there was very little commotion. Occasionally a man's deep voice or a woman's tinkling giggle could be heard above the music. Otherwise, though everyone appeared to be having fun, the atmosphere felt quietly restrained.

David was seated between Sally and Dillon at a large, round table along with Sally's parents, Dillon's parents, and Gray. The adults were doing most of the talking, which was fine with David, who was happy to concentrate on his food. The mood was celebratory, with lots of toasts offered in honor of Gray's election to the Hall of Fame, the St. Matthew's victory, and David's game-winning touchdown.

Dillon seemed to have settled into a deep funk, but David was nevertheless enjoying himself. At Mr. Dillon's urging he had ordered a T-bone steak and devoured all sixteen ounces of it, along with his clam chowder, baked potato, and salad. When the waiter appeared to whisk away their dinner plates David was sure he didn't have room for one more bite.

But Mr. Dillon wouldn't hear of his not ordering a dessert. "We'll look at the dessert cart," he told the waiter with a chuckle, "since dinner is on Mr. Wheeler here."

Sally's father smiled and folded his hands on top of the white linen tablecloth. "I consider it a moral victory. It could have gone either way," he said.

"There is no column in the record book for the moral victories," Mr. Dillon reminded him. "How do you like our little club, David?"

"It's unbelievable," David said, wishing Sally would quit kicking his foot under the table. "In Scranton, a club is three guys who chip in to buy an old Buick."

Mr. Dillon laughed, a deep, hearty laugh that rumbled across the room. The others, except for his son, joined in with him. "Good arm, good sense of humor. Not a bad combination," he said with an approving nod.

David smiled. "I wasn't being funny."

His honesty provoked even more laughter. Mrs. Wheeler beamed at her daughter. Her young man was utterly sweet and charming.

A man of about Mr. Dillon's age stopped at the table and said, "Hello, Grayson."

"Tom Keating, how are you? See the game?" inquired Mr. Dillon.

"I wouldn't have missed it for the world," the other man said, slightly slurring his words. "That new quarterback is the great white hope, isn't he?"

"Yes, and you can shake his hand. David Greene, this is Mr. Keating, one of our trustees."

"Son, on behalf of the old guard, many thanks. It's good to be a winner again." Mr. Keating took a step forward and had to grab hold of the back of David's chair to keep from stumbling.

"You know the Wheelers," Mr. Dillon said.

"Yes, hello again." Mr. Keating nodded.

"And my boys, Gray and Charlie."

"Of course. Congratulations, Gray, quite an honor."

"Call me in the city, Tom, we'll get together," said Mr. Dillon.

"I'll do that, Grayson. Have a nice evening," Mr. Keating said, smiling crookedly. "Gray, I'd like to introduce you to someone. Do you mind?"

Gray stood up and grinned at his family, acknowledging the demands of celebrity. He followed Mr. Keating, who seemed to be listing slightly to one side.

"I believe Tom Keating has had a drink or two," said Mrs. Dillon, primly stating the obvious.

Mrs. Wheeler sighed. "He does have that problem."

"Remember that time he brought a Jew lawyer here from Boston for a round of golf?" asked Mr. Wheeler. He made a face and took a long sip of water, as if to wash away the bad taste left there by the memory.

Mr. Dillon cleared his throat, seemed about to speak, then changed his mind. He picked up his dessert fork and tapped it gently against the tabletop.

"They never made it to the first tee," Mr. Wheeler went on, appearing not to notice his friend's rather obvious discomfort with the direction of his remarks. "I've never understood the fascination with Jew lawyers. It's not like they're cheap."

His guests laughed appreciatively at his insight, and Grayson Dillon managed a weak chuckle.

Even David found himself joining in the merriment.

"Excuse me," said Dillon's mother, glancing across the room. She stood up from the table. "I see Mrs. Bartram left unattended. Please, don't get up."

"How about a dance?" Mr. Wheeler asked his wife.

"If one of these young men would dance with Sally," Mrs. Wheeler said coyly.

"Mother!" Sally hissed.

Happy for an excuse to leave the table and be alone with Sally, Dillon pushed back his chair. But his father put out a restraining hand and said, "David, do you mind? I'd like to have a word with this guy."

David glanced from Dillon to Sally. Then, working hard to keep his expression neutral, he said, "Would you like to dance?"

"Sure," Sally said as casually as she could manage.

He nodded. "Okay."

Suppressing their smiles, they headed for the dance floor. After several minutes of subtle maneuvering they managed to put enough distance between themselves and the other couples that they could talk privately.

"I have a secret," Sally said, brushing her hair lightly against David's cheek. "I think about you . . . a lot more than I ought to."

David breathed in lilacs. He was longing to put his arms around her and hug her, right here in front of everyone. Instead he said, "That's too bad."

She flashed him a strange look. He realized his teasing had scared her, so he squeezed her hand and quickly continued. "Because if you think of me as much as I think of you, we're both going to flunk right out of school."

"Am I all sweaty and red in the face?" Sally said, dancing as close to him as she dared.

He looked at her, then looked away. Her face was so beautiful. He could hardly bear not to kiss her. "You look like an angel," he said.

They followed the rhythm of the music for a moment or two. Then she said, "What are you looking at?"

"Poor Dillon. He looks like he's dying."

"If you mention Charlie Dillon once more, I will sit down in a huff." She pouted and twirled away from him. When she came back into his arms she said, "I will, too. You know I'm a spoiled brat."

"Dillon, Dillon, Dillon," David chanted. "Charlie, Charlie, Charlie."

Sally loved that he was teasing her. He was so dreamy—smart, handsome, and not a bit stuck up just because he was a football hero. She pulled him closer, not caring now who saw them. She was almost seventeen, old enough to decide what she should or shouldn't do with the boy she loved. And what she really wanted to do, she realized, was kiss him. That having been decided, she stopped dancing, took his arm, and led him out onto the terrace.

Inside, Dillon was wishing like crazy that his father would get to the point of their heart-to-heart talk. "Son, you played a good game today," his father was saying.

"Not as good as some people," Dillon said sullenly.

"Don't sell yourself short. That was a key block. Without your block David couldn't have scored."

Dillon squirmed in his seat and craned his neck, searching the room for Sally. He knew his father was trying to cheer him up, but his lecture was having exactly the opposite effect. Dillon was no dope. He could smell the bullshit when it got dumped in front of him. The only thing that would cheer him up would be a long, slow dance with his girl.

"Charlie, listen to me," his father persisted. "Don't let your brother's award take anything away from your day."

"No, of course not," Dillon said petulantly. He picked up the salt shaker and poured until he had created a tiny mound in front of his place. "I threw a good block, he got into the Hall of Fame."

"People have different natural abilities."

"In other words, I should accept my mediocrity," Dillon replied with a bitter laugh. He swirled the tines of his fork through the salt and examined the design he'd created.

"You are *not* mediocre. You wouldn't be at St. Matt's if you were," said his father, resorting to logic. "Look, you guys beat St. Luke's. Nobody thought you had a chance. Enjoy it."

"All right, fine." Dillon threw down the fork. "I'm enjoying it. Can I go now?"

His father gave up with a sigh and nodded his permission. Dillon read his expression: The boy was impossible. There was no use trying to tell him anything.

It was cold outside, but David and Sally didn't feel the chill. They stood in each other's arms, warmed by the excitement of the feelings they were discovering. All their yearnings and desires were reflected in their eyes as they pressed cheek against cheek and swayed to the music. Sally leaned her head up to David. Their lips were just on the verge of meeting in a kiss when Dillon stepped out of the shadows.

He stood watching them for a moment. Then he grabbed Sally's hand and said to David, "Thanks for taking care of my girl."

"Stop saying that!" Sally jerked her hand away. Positioning herself between the two boys, she defied Dillon to claim her. "I am *not* your girl," she angrily informed him.

Her outburst dropped like a bomb on the unsuspecting Dillon. "What the hell is this?" he demanded.

"You don't listen very well, do you?" said Sally, flicking her hair off her face.

"C'mon, Sally, you're embarrassing me in front of my friend. Let's go have a talk," Dillon urged, and he tried to take her hand again.

But she slapped him away. "No, you're embarrassing *me* in front of *my* friend," she said, deliberately choosing the words that she knew would

158

wound him. Then she just as deliberately turned her back on Dillon and smiled an apology at David.

David felt the situation sliding out of control. He had never meant to fall for Sally, never meant to take her away from Dillon. Besides, she had told him she wasn't Dillon's girl. But the hurt and anger on Dillon's face were too obvious to ignore.

"Charlie," he said, groping for the words to make things better between them, "it just kind of happened."

"Screw you, *friend!*" spat Dillon.

David started to go after him, but Sally held him back. "Let him go," she said.

His impulse was to chase Dillon down and try to explain. But what would he say that would make any kind of difference? That he was willing to give Sally up? No way. He couldn't do that, not even for Dillon.

"I know him," Sally said firmly, entwining her fingers with his. "He just needs time to cool off. I'll speak to him later."

Her hands felt cold, so he brought them up against his chest to warm them beneath his jacket. Sally nestled closer and stared up into his eyes. The invitation couldn't have been clearer. But as he bent his head to kiss her, Sally took his face in her hands and studied him feature by feature.

David hoped that whatever she was looking for, he had it for her to discover. He so badly wanted to be what she wanted, for her to become a part of his life. The intensity of his desire was a new and troubling feeling. It almost hurt to have her look at him so closely, and he knew intuitively that only the touch of her lips against his would relieve that hurt.

Then he kissed her, a kiss that he wished could go on forever, and he was quite sure that nothing would ever again be the same between them.

Dillon stalked back inside and went straight to the bar. His brother and Mr. Keating were chatting over their drinks with a third man whom he didn't recognize.

"To the victors!" Mr. Keating toasted, raising his glass. "Where's your friend?"

"What friend?" Dillon snapped. "Do I get a drink?"

Gray heard the fury in his brother's voice and thought twice about reminding him to stick to Coke or ginger ale.

"Absolutely!" said Mr. Keating, who'd had too many to consider whether or not Dillon was legally old enough to drink.

"Scotch 'n' soda," said Dillon.

Mr. Keating cocked an eyebrow at his companions. Then he gave the order to the bartender. "Dewar's and soda." Turning back to Dillon, he asked, "You ever meet Cal Reynolds, Charlie? Class of '21?"

"No, how do you do?" Dillon said, trying to sound civil.

"Hi, Charlie. Congratulations," said Mr. Reynolds.

"St. *Luke's* class of '21," Mr. Keating explained. "That's why he looks so down in the mouth."

Mr. Reynolds smiled. "I wish we had found that Greene kid first," he said.

"Why?" Mr. Keating threw back what was left of his scotch and guffawed. "St. Luke's wouldn't have taken him."

"No, probably not," agreed Mr. Reynolds.

"Ah, your drink." Mr. Keating handed Dillon his glass.

Dillon took a sip of the scotch and tried not to make a face as the alcohol burned the back of his throat. "Why wouldn't St. Luke's take him?" he wanted to know.

"Greene?" Mr. Reynolds cracked up as if Dillon had just told him a hilariously funny story. When he finally stopped laughing he said, "They wouldn't have enrolled a Jew, not even for a championship."

Gray almost choked on his drink. "A Jew?" he sputtered.

"A Jew!" Dillon glared at Mr. Reynolds for having the poor taste to joke about St. Matthew's honor.

But Mr. Keating's response confirmed that the other man was telling the truth. "Reynolds, have I told you how nicely you keep a secret?"

"Holy shit!" Dillon swore softly.

"Sorry," Mr. Reynolds apologized, looking as though he wished he'd bitten his tongue.

Too shocked to speak, Dillon sat down on a bar stool to mull over this amazing disclosure. A great many pieces of the puzzle fell into place. He had always sensed there was something different about Greene, but he'd chalked it up to his coming from a public school in Scranton. Trust a Jew to think he could fit right in, take over the team, steal his girl. But what burned Dillon most was that the bastard had lied to all of them. And for that he was going to pay. Dillon would see to it.

9

V an Kelt spat the toothpaste out of his mouth and grumbled into the mirror, "I can't believe I dropped that pass in the end zone."

"Neither can I," came Reece's voice from the communal shower stalls across from the sinks.

"That's it, punish me," said Van Kelt in a mock-tragic tone.

"Suffer," Reece taunted him good-naturedly.

David flicked a spray of water at Reece and called out, "Forget it, Rip. We won."

Reece was about to step out of the shower when Dillon walked in. David tensed, waiting for Dillon to give him a hard time about Sally. But Reece, who'd heard about the fight from David, quickly said, "Hey, Dillon, what a block, boy."

"I taught him all he knows," yelled Van Kelt, soaping his face.

Dillon rolled his eyes as he turned on one of the

vacant faucets. "God save me," he said melodramatically.

David relaxed. Dillon seemed okay, like maybe he was ready to forgive and forget. "You did play a great game, Dillon," he said, hoping to break the ice between them.

"We beat St. Luke's," said Dillon. He glanced sideways at David. "That was the grand plan."

"Yeah!" shouted Reece.

"Mission accomplished. The old boy network got together and bought us a victory," Dillon said sourly. He reached for the soap and added, "But the joke's on us."

Van Kelt turned off the water at his sink so he could hear better. "What joke?" he asked.

"You didn't hear the joke?" said Dillon.

"Okay," Reece said, sounding as if he were talking to a child. "Let's hear the joke."

"True story," Dillon assured the other boys. He poured shampoo into his hair and lathered the suds. "Last weekend there was a religious revival at Madison Square Garden. Bishop Fulton Sheen gave a stirring address, and afterwards ten thousand people converted to Catholicism."

Van Kelt, who didn't want to miss the punch line, appeared in the doorway of the shower.

"But then Billy Graham got up, and after half an hour of inspired preaching ten thousand people converted to Protestantism," Dillon continued. "Finally, to end the program, Pat Boone got up and sang, 'There's a Gold Mine in the Sky.'" Dillon paused and pretended to wipe soap from his eyes. "Twenty thousand Jews joined the air force."

His audience was convulsed with laughter—all but David, who immediately understood the message behind Dillon's meanness.

"What's the matter, Greene?" Dillon taunted him. "Don't the Jews have a sense of humor?"

Confused by Dillon's gibes, the other boys looked from him to David, who glared silently at Dillon.

"Yeah, well." Dillon shrugged. "It turns out our golden boy here is a dirty, lying kike."

All the insults and slurs David had overlooked, all the comebacks he'd swallowed since his first day at St. Matthew's suddenly exploded in his brain like a megaton bomb. He reacted without thinking to Dillon's use of that one terrible word he hated more than any other. His fist flew up and slammed into Dillon's jaw, pitching Dillon off balance. Dillon grabbed for him as he fell. Then the two of them were on the floor of the shower, wrestling and poking at each other through the steam and pelting water.

"Get the door," yelled Van Kelt.

One of the other boys ran to lock the bathroom door. While their friends looked on, speechless, David and Dillon rolled across the wet tile, screaming and grunting with rage. Finally David managed to pull Dillon up and push him away.

"I don't want to fight you," he shouted.

"Go ahead, deny it!" screamed Dillon.

David shook his head.

"See! It's true! It's true! He's a hebe!" Dillon screamed.

He sprang at David, but David was quicker. He

Deborah Chiel

got in three sharp jabs that sent Dillon flying to the floor. He threw up his fists for round two, but the others had seen enough. Reece grabbed his arms and pulled him away. Van Kelt put out a hand to help Dillon to his feet.

Nobody said a word. But David didn't have to work very hard to guess what they were all thinking.

Reece was sitting at his desk, his lips compressed in a tight, angry line, his nose stuck in a chemistry book. He'd been quiet the whole time he'd toweled himself off in the bathroom, walked back down the hall to their room, and changed into his pajamas. The silent treatment was starting to drive David crazy. He could imagine Chesty or Magoo behaving like creeps, but not Reece.

He opened his drawer and pulled out the Band-Aid box he'd stuck away there in September. No more hiding, he told himself as he extricated his Star of David. From now on he wasn't going to hide a goddamn thing from anyone. But that didn't solve the problem of Reece ignoring him.

"You gonna keep your face in a book for the rest of the year?" he said, gripping the star in his hand.

Reece looked up and finally met his eye. "What do you expect me to say?"

"That it's no big deal." Though the window was open and it was cool in the room, David could feel the sweat trickling down his back.

Reece threw the book down on his desk. "If it's no big deal, why didn't you tell me in the first place? I am your roommate."

166

David fastened around his neck the chain from which the Star of David hung. The weight felt familiar and comfortable. "You never told me what religion you are." He turned to face his roommate so Reece could see the six-pointed star.

"I'm Methodist."

"You're Methodist? And all the time I didn't know." David tried to make a joke, but his voice turned bitter around the edges.

"That's different," said Reece.

"How is it different?"

"It just is. Jews are different. It's not like between Methodists and Lutherans. I mean, Jews . . . everything about them is . . . different."

"Okay, let's get it out," David said. Too angry to sit still, he stood up and paced the room. "You think Jews are dirt, right?"

"Come on, David, nobody said—"

"No, *you* come on. If you're gonna be like them, say it to my face," David shouted. "Let it out! Say it! Jews are greedy, money-grubbing—"

"Come off it!" Reece yelled.

David took a deep breath. As hurt as he was, he could see that Reece was hurting, too. He wasn't sure which bothered Reece more—the fact that David was Jewish, or that he'd kept his religion a secret even from his roommate. The least he could do was try and make Reece understand why he'd kept it hidden.

"The first day I came to this place I thought I was dreaming. I was only going to be here for a year, but I thought, man, what a year," he began, figuring it out for himself as he went along. "I'd get into

Harvard, which isn't all that easy if you come from Podunk Public High School. All you guys were my friends, we were winning games, I met Sally . . ."

Suddenly scared that things might now change between himself and Sally, David sank down onto his bed. "I didn't want anything to mess it up," he went on, unsure that Reece could grasp his dilemma. "I didn't want to be told I couldn't be a part of it because I was a Jew. It's happened before. Can you understand that?"

"You could have told us. It wouldn't have made any difference," Reece insisted.

"Sure, Reece," David said sarcastically. "I knew that the first night I got here, when I heard how McGivern got his hi-fi. Remember? He jewed him down."

Reece didn't respond, but the look of shame on his face told David he remembered.

"Sure, it wouldn't have made any difference," David said. He took off his bathrobe, dropped it on the floor, and crawled under the covers. He was wasting his breath. It was no use. Reece would never get it. He had been born an insider. He could never be made to understand how it felt to be on the outside, looking in at the world he took for granted. That was a hard, ugly truth, and why would Reece—or anyone else, for that matter— ever want to face it?

All through Sunday and into Monday a cold, relentless rain poured down, which perfectly suited David's dark, angry mood. He and Reece exchanged only the words they had to as roommates.

The rest of the crowd, led by Dillon, wouldn't even look at him, let alone say hello.

David could never have imagined feeling so lonely or friendless. If it hadn't been that the Thanksgiving break was only two days away, he might have followed his heart and jumped on the first bus back to Scranton.

On Monday morning, when David walked into the foyer to check his mail, the other boys already gathered there suddenly fell away to create a huge, empty space around him. He wanted to ask them if they were worried that they might be contaminated by his presence if they got too close. Instead he gritted his teeth and pretended they weren't there.

He opened his mailbox and found, alongside a letter from his sister, a rough wooden cross. Cheap shot, he thought. He would have expected a more sophisticated trick from this crowd.

Determined to keep his cool, he turned and dangled the cross in front of their faces. His own face was a mask. No way was he going to give them even a clue to what he was feeling. He dropped the cross in the outgoing mail slot and grimly went off by himself to French, his first class of the day.

For once he was grateful for Mr. Cleary's interminable drills and recitations. His entire brain was focused on spitting out the right answer whenever Mr. Cleary pointed a ruler in his direction. Today, however, even Mr. Cleary seemed less intent on destroying his students' egos. Though he still went after those who had shown up unprepared, without McGivern there to be his handpicked target, Mr. Cleary had lost some of his venom.

The class bell rang, and the boys gathered up their books and got ready to leave.

"One moment, please," said Mr. Cleary. He reached into his briefcase and pulled out a stack of blue exam books. "I've graded your take-home translations," he announced.

A low groan swept through the room.

"They weren't all that bad," Mr. Cleary said. "Mr. Connors, especially, wrote a nearly flawless translation."

Connors grinned with relief. He'd worked like the devil on that exam.

"I noticed, Mr. Connors, like the rest of the class, you signed the honor code agreement," Mr. Cleary said.

Something about Mr. Cleary's comment made Connors nervous. "Yeah?" he replied, no longer smiling.

"Which indicates a promise not to cheat in any way."

"Yeah?" Connors said again, his voice rising.

"The use of a published translation would be cheating, would it not?" asked Mr. Cleary.

Connors's normally ruddy complexion had turned fire-engine red. "I didn't use anything but a dictionary," he protested.

"If you say so," conceded Mr. Cleary, implying by his tone that Connors must surely be lying. "Your translation, however, was a quantum leap over your previous efforts."

"Must be because you're such a great teacher, *sir,*" Connors shot back.

He won the round.

Mr. Cleary tossed the blue books across his desk. "Pick up your graded papers," he said, and he left the room.

The boys rushed up to his desk, grabbed their exams, and hurried out after him. Only Connors remained seated, too irate to move. David walked over and put a sympathetic hand on his shoulder. But Connors shook him off, got up, and stomped out of the room without picking up his blue book.

David and Reece were the only ones left in the classroom. "How'd you do?" Reece asked, nervously jingling the change in his pocket.

"B," said David.

"Me, too."

"Aren't you afraid of being seen with me?" David asked, not bothering to disguise his rancor.

Reece was clearly uncomfortable with David's belligerence. "I've known these guys for four years," he said, fanning his blue book. "They're not bad guys, David. Just give them a little time."

"Sure," David said, wondering which of them was the bigger liar.

David hadn't heard from Sally since he'd said good-bye to her outside the country club on Saturday night. He made up a long list of excuses why she hadn't been in touch—until it dawned on him that *he* was the one who was supposed to be calling *her*. Boy, was he a fool! She was probably standing by the phone in her dorm, praying that he would give her a ring.

There was a long line at the pay phone until just before lights out. David dialed her number, asked the girl at the other end to call Sally Wheeler, and held his breath while he waited for her to pick up. "C'mon . . . c'mon . . ." he mumbled into the receiver.

Mr. Cleary, as usual, was prowling the halls. He noticed David standing at the end of the corridor and tapped his watch to remind him of the time. David nodded. He'd talk fast.

"Hello?" came the voice at the other end.

"Hello?" David's heart was beating a rapid tattoo. "Sally?"

"I'm sorry, she isn't in right now," said the girl.

"I *know* she's there. Tell her I have to talk to her, please. It's very important," David pleaded.

He heard the girl sigh. Then she said, "Hold on."

A minute later she was back. "I'm sorry, she won't speak to you," the girl told him, sounding genuinely regretful. "She said please don't call her again. I'm sorry."

He heard a click. The girl had hung up. *But what about how we felt together?* David mentally sent a message to Sally across the miles of telephone wires. *Doesn't that count for anything?*

Apparently not. A dial tone buzzed in David's ear. The connection had been broken.

The rain mixed with sleet continued to fall through most of Tuesday. David slogged through the mud from one class to the next, too miserable to notice the cold and wet. Now that the football season was over, David was glad not to have to face his teammates in the locker room. He spent the extra time in the library, avoiding their snide comments and hostile stares.

But he couldn't avoid them in the dining room, where he had to fulfill their requests. All through dinner they'd had him hustling between the kitchen and their table, piling on the demands as if he were some feelingless robot who'd been specially created to do their bidding. He came close to hurling the dessert plates onto the table.

"Ah-Jew!" cried Magoo, pretending to sneeze.

Chesty, Connors, and Dillon snickered. "Grow up, for crissake," muttered Reece.

"Oh, Reece," sniffed Magoo. "You're so mature."

Dillon snapped his fingers at David and said, *"Garçon, plus d'eau, s'il vous plaît."*

David fought the impulse to smash a plate over Dillon's head and instead went off to get more water. While he was gone Magoo grabbed the opportunity to stick the salt shaker in his pocket.

"Excuse me, there's no salt on this table," he haughtily informed David when he returned with a fresh pitcher of water. "I need salt for my pie. Someone's not doing his menial job."

"It's so hard to get decent help these days." Chesty threw in his two cents.

"Gentlemen, watch your behavior." Mr. Swanson scolded them.

"Can't you move any faster?" Magoo complained.

"Collins!" Mr. Swanson warned.

David decided he had taken enough crap from Magoo. He slammed the pitcher down on the table with such force that water splashed over the sides. "You want to step outside, I'll show you how fast I can move," he told Magoo, shaking his finger directly in front of Magoo's thick glasses.

"That's a threat!" Magoo yelled. "You all heard it. He threatened me!"

"Shut up, Magoo," said Reece. He pushed David away from the table and told him, "It's not worth it."

"My name is Richard Collins. What's yours— Greenberg?" jeered Magoo.

Reece shook his head. He was fed up with Magoo's junior high school humor. The guy was way out of line.

But he had managed to provoke David, who barged into the kitchen and whipped off his white jacket. Miller, another of the waiters, came in right behind him. "I'll work that table. You can take mine," he offered. "You need this job, same as I do."

David hesitated. He and Miller were in the same history class, but he barely knew him. Still, he'd always seemed like a nice enough guy.

"C'mon Greene. Don't blow it. Things will cool down over Thanksgiving," Miller said.

"All right, thanks." David nodded. That assumed, of course, that he would come back after Thanksgiving. But he wouldn't think about that until he got home. Now he had a shift to finish.

* * *

SCHOOL TIES

His whole family was waiting for David when his bus arrived at the Scranton terminal. He was dressed the way he'd gotten used to dressing at school, in his khaki pants, white bucks, and new short haircut. Sharp-eyed Sarah noticed the difference as soon as he came down the steps.

"Excuse me, was my brother on that bus? His name is David Greene," she teased, throwing her arms around him.

He'd thought about pulling his old duds out of the back of the closet. But the same clothes that had felt so comfortable just last summer no longer fit him—or maybe they didn't fit the person he'd grown used to being.

"You look great, David," his father assured him. "Let's get you home."

"Yeah, before anybody sees him," joked Petey, whose face was creased in an ear-to-ear grin. He couldn't wait to have David all to himself, to hear about every single one of David's amazing passes and touchdowns.

"Never thought I'd be happy to smell sulphur," said David, pulling his sister's hair.

"Are you a hero there yet?" Petey asked.

A typical Petey question, but it caught David unawares. Some hero, David thought. He wrapped one arm around Petey's neck and grabbed him up in a hug.

"I'm working on it," he told his little brother.

His house looked small and shabby after the far more elegantly decorated public rooms of Iselin Hall. But it felt great to be home, to sprawl on the living room floor in front of the TV, to prowl around the kitchen at midnight when he suddenly got hungry for a chicken sandwich on rye.

He slept past noon on Thanksgiving morning and came downstairs to find Sarah stuffing the turkey so she could get it into the oven in time for dinner. On her way home from the bus station she'd bragged that she'd spent every afternoon that week making chopped liver and baking cookies, pies, and noodle pudding. The refrigerator bulged with the proof of her efforts.

David waited for her to tease him again about his wardrobe, because he was dressed this morning in an oxford shirt, a blue crewneck, and his khakis. But Sarah was distracted with the cooking. She handed him a glass of juice and a plate of toast and shooed him out of her way.

Petey and Pop were planted in front of the TV, watching the Army–Navy game. David sat with them for a couple of minutes until he finished the toast. Then he went off to make a phone call. He'd thought about this the whole way back from school. Sally *had* to talk to him. If he called her at home, her mother was sure to remember him and make Sally pick up the phone.

He stretched the cord from the kitchen phone as far as it would go into the hallway. The TV was blaring in the background, and Sarah was shouting at Petey to come take out the garbage. But if he waited until he had quiet and privacy, he'd have to phone Sally in the middle of the night.

His palms were sweaty as he dialed Sally's number. Nothing to be nervous about, he told himself. Once he had the chance to talk to Sally, she'd stop being mad at him, and they could continue where they'd left off after Homecoming.

Mrs. Wheeler picked up on the third ring, but it took her a while to recall who he was. "We met at the St. Luke's game? And had dinner and everything?" he reminded her. "Anyway, I was wondering if I could talk to Sally . . . Do you know when she'll be back? . . . I see."

Excuses. That's all he was hearing. He wasn't even sure if Mrs. Wheeler was telling the truth. Probably Sally was standing right there, listening to her mother's lies. "Yeah, I think I understand," he said finally. "I think I understand pretty well."

He hung up the phone and slouched back into the living room. Petey was adjusting the rabbit ears on top of the TV set.

"Little to the left," his father directed him. "Good. Perfect."

David stared restlessly at the shadowy images on the screen. As soon as Petey let go of the antenna the picture turned snowy again.

"You gotta hold it, Petey," said his father.

"I don't want to hold it," Petey objected. "I wanna watch it."

"How's the game?" asked David.

"Navy all the way. It's a little boring," his father said.

"Could I have the car?"

His father shifted in his chair, dug in his pocket for the keys, and flipped them to David. "Back for dinner, and in one piece," he said, same as he did every time he let David borrow the car.

David smiled wanly. Now he *knew* he was home.

"Can I come?" Petey begged.

David shrugged. Why not? It took so little to make Petey happy.

The mine was closed for the holiday. The equipment lay idle, intruding upon the drab, monochromatic landscape like hideous metallic monsters on the face of the moon. Beyond the mine the streets all looked the same. Nothing had changed since he'd left. The town lacked the charm he'd become accustomed to in Massachusetts. It felt small and confining, lacking any spirit or hope.

Petey was watching his every move, making car noises in his throat, pretending to downshift and steer and brake just like David. "Whatcha looking at?" he asked.

"I don't know," said David. But he did know. He was looking for any small sign of cheer, of freshness or color. He couldn't find it anywhere around him.

He hadn't planned to stop at Edie's, but when he saw the usual crowd loitering in front he changed his mind and pulled over. Looking as if he might burst with pride, Petey followed him inside.

Bear was there, grinning and pointing to the cast that extended from his right ankle to his knee. Don and Nick were seated across from him in their usual booth, chain-smoking and sucking on their Coke straws.

Edie had to give David a hug and a free Coke. But before he could drink it he had to sign Bear's cast.

"Tough break," he scrawled. "Love, David Greene."

Petey went off to investigate the pinball machine, and finally David was free to join his friends. Just like old times, he thought, and he helped himself to one of Bear's french fries. Then he wanted to hear how Bear had gotten so banged up, and Bear was pleased to oblige.

He'd missed seeing a deep rut in the road that forked off just behind the mine, he explained. "The Harley held up pretty good, but I don't know, the old leg took a lickin'. Penn State let me know they don't want a gimpy linebacker."

"I'm sorry, Bear," David said. He knew that Bear's chance to go to college had disappeared along with the football scholarship.

"No big deal. The navy'll take me. I'll see the world."

Joyce and Mary Ellen stopped by the booth. Mary Ellen hardly glanced at Bear, and David wondered when they'd broken up.

"Hi, Davy," said Joyce, pulling off the kerchief she'd worn to protect her hair from the wind. "In for the weekend?"

"Yeah. Hi, Joyce. Hi, Mary Ellen."

"Gee, you look different," said Joyce.

"Very collegiate." Mary Ellen giggled.

David watched them walk past. Compared to Sally, they both seemed pale and dull.

"You hear about Stauffer?" said Don.

"What about him?"

Bear lit another cigarette. "He knocked up Eileen. Now they're married."

"Married? They can't be," said David. "They're still in high school."

"Not anymore," Nick said.

"They're livin' with her mother. He's workin' full time at Purolator, makin' them oil filters at ninety-five cents an hour." Bear shifted his leg and tried to get more comfortable. "She's home with mama gettin' fat."

David tried to imagine Eileen, who had always talked about becoming a nurse, married to Stauffer, and the two of them about to become parents. "Wow. Drop dead twice."

"Yeah," said Bear.

There was a moment of silence, as if they were all giving thanks that they weren't in Stauffer's place. Then David said, "How's school?"

Don threw him a puzzled glance. "Whaddaya mean?"

"How is it? How's it going?"

"School?" Don shrugged. "It's closed for the long weekend."

"School is school," said Nick, unwrapping a stick of gum.

"School is for the birds," said Bear.

"I woulda quit, but the old lady wouldn't sign," Don explained.

Joyce had pulled Mary Ellen out of their booth, and now they were dancing to the song on the jukebox. The boys watched them as they tried out the steps they'd just seen on "American Bandstand."

"She said one more year wouldn't kill me," said Don, slumping against the back of the booth. "Hope she's right."

"My cousin said she might get me in at the A 'n' P," Nick said, chomping loudly on his gum. "Thirty-five skins a week, and all you can steal."

Bear waved his hand dismissively. He had it all figured out. "The navy's better, man. Three squares a day and a flop. Medical, dental—"

"Yeah," laughed Don. "Barfin' your guts out over the North Atlantic. Me, I'm headin' for Philly. Standard Pressed Steel. They're hirin' again."

"Philly's great, only if you love niggers," said Nick.

"I got nothin' against niggers," Don said. "They're human beings just like the rest of us."

"You want one marryin' your sister?"

"Yeah." Don picked up his fork and speared a pickle chip. Halfway to his mouth he dropped the fork, as if he were too exhausted to complete the motion.

"You wanna marry one your own self?" Bear asked incredulously.

"I don't wanna marry nobody." Don set the record straight. "I want to be wild as the wind. When I go to that old graveyard, I want it on my tombstone: 'He really lived life.'"

Working the line at Standard Pressed meant twenty-five years of soul-deadening boredom until he earned his pension. The best Don had to look forward to was a six-pack on Friday night, a hangover on Saturday, and a chance to score before Monday rolled around. The utter irony of his dream struck David to the core.

But even more chilling was the realization that

he didn't belong here any more than he belonged at St. Matthew's.

David was determined not to ruin his family reunion by bringing all his problems to the table. Somehow he was able to fake his way through Thanksgiving dinner. He took second helpings of everything, told Sarah she was getting to be almost as good a cook as Mom, and regaled Petey with detailed descriptions of every game he'd played that season.

But inside he was aching so badly that he wished he were five years old again and his mother were alive so he could fling himself in her lap for comfort.

Only Pop wasn't fooled. He waited until after dinner, when the dishes were done, and he and David were taking out the garbage. "Okay, out with it," he said as they walked out onto the back porch, where Petey's bike and the old washing machine were stored.

"What?" said David.

"You tell me. Your face was on the floor all during dinner. Hell, since you came home."

"It's school. Maybe that was a mistake."

"What happened?" his father asked.

David looked up at the sky. A very bright, full moon shone among the winter constellations, lighting a path across the lawn.

"Maybe I shouldn't be there," David said, hating himself for breaking his father's heart. "I don't fit in. I don't fit in here anymore. I don't know where I fit in."

"I thought you loved the place," his father said, lifting the top to the garbage can.

For the first time since his mother had died David felt himself on the verge of tears. "Pop," he said, his voice breaking, "I shouldn't have gone there."

"What happened? Something happened."

David groped to explain the inexplicable. How could Pop understand? All he knew was Scranton. The rest of the world remained a mystery to be solved and interpreted by his oldest son. "I got a taste of something there that I really liked, that I really wanted. Something I thought I could have."

"Please, David, I'm a simple man." His father pressed down the garbage with his clenched fist and replaced the lids with a loud clang. "What are you saying?"

He fought to hold back the tears that were stinging his eyes. "I did something awful." He began slowly. Then, eager to clear his conscience and tell his father the worst, David forced the words out in a stream of confession. "I pretended I wasn't Jewish. I wasn't planning to. It just happened. I somehow got in with them. I was trying so hard. There was never a good time to . . . Then I was afraid to say anything because it was too late!"

"And they found out."

David nodded. The wind whistled through the trees, bringing with it the odor of the mines.

"I should have told you. It's not like I don't know," his father said, sounding as if he, too, was on the verge of tears. "When you go somewhere, *anywhere,* and the people there don't know you, first thing out of your mouth, you gotta say, 'I am a Jew.'"

He paused to let the words sink in. Then he continued, "Loud and clear. You say it in your own words, in your own way, but you *say* it. You let them know that. Then you start belonging or not belonging on your terms, as a Jew. I should have told you that, but—"

"But you never thought I would hide it." David finished his sentence.

"That's right," his father bitterly agreed. "I never thought you would hide it."

"I was sick of fighting," said David. And you told me not to fight, he thought. You told me to fit in. Why didn't you tell me I could fit in *and* be a Jew?

"I can't make you go back. If I could force you, if I could stand over you with a whip . . ." Alan Greene shook his head and turned to go back to the house. "But some things a person has to decide for himself."

David didn't follow his father inside. He needed to be alone to sort out his feelings. He sat down on the porch steps and listened to all the voices in his head battling to be heard. Grandpa, Pop, Kocus, Dr. Bartram, Coach McDevitt, Dillon, Reece . . . Each one of them believed he knew the truth. Each one of them thought his own way was best.

But the truth was they were all fighting their own battles, not his. And whether they were right or wrong, fair-minded or bigots, they'd made up their minds the only way they could. Trial and error. Bitter experience. Living their lives and making their own mistakes.

Some things a person had to decide for himself what to do. He could agree with Pop, or he could decide not to agree with him. Ultimately it was his life. He had to cut his own path through the forest of infinite possibilities. He couldn't let himself be sidetracked by anyone else's hopes or prejudices.

His father stood in the door, watching him as he walked up the stairs.

"They can't make me disappear," David said.

He was allowed to mess up, just like everybody else. The worst thing would be to give up because he hadn't gotten it absolutely right the first time out. He *was* different from the rest of the boys at St. Matthew's, and he was proud of that difference, even if it set him apart. But he was like them, too. He'd spent too many hours talking things over with Reece and Dillon and McGivern not to believe that. And he belonged there, just the same as they did.

10

No one was waiting to meet David's bus when he returned from the Thanksgiving holiday. The rain was still coming down, and his taxi almost had to swim up the hill to the campus. It took every ounce of David's resolve to walk into the dorm and down the corridor where a hot game of hall hockey was in progress. Dillon, Connors, Van Kelt, and a few of the others were noisily batting a wadded-up piece of paper toward the overturned wastebaskets at either end of the hall.

Their cries and shouts stopped as soon as they saw him. But nobody said hello. Had they thought he wasn't coming back? Did they think their silence could freeze him out of the school?

If so, he would show them how strong he could be. Let them ignore him. They believed they were the only boys who counted at St. Matthew's, but there had to be others who weren't so sure they had life all figured out.

There was nothing they could do to change his mind about staying in school. Or so he thought until he walked into his room the next day. He stared in horror at the sign hanging on the wall above his bed. He wanted to run, to get as far away as possible from the picture of the blood-red swastika. "GO HOME, JEW!" screamed the heavy black print below the swastika.

Grandpa and his Hebrew school teachers had talked about the terrible symbolism of the swastika, adopted by Hitler and his Nazi followers, who had systematically murdered millions of European Jews during World War II. But this was America. It was his home, and goddammit, he wasn't going anywhere.

He ripped a page out of his notebook and scribbled his answer to the sick bastards who thought he could be so easily intimidated. WHOEVER MADE THE SIGN CAN MEET ME TONIGHT AT 10:30 BEHIND ISELIN HALL.

He was sick of fighting, but what choice did he have?

Some boys had gathered in the hall outside his room. If they were waiting to see his reaction, they didn't have to wait long. He thumbtacked the sign to the wall and walked away.

The rain hadn't stopped. Whipped by the wind, it fell sideways, an icy torrent that stung David's cheeks as he took up his post behind the dorm. The lights were dimming across the campus, and he could hear an occasional faint call of "Lights out!"

He had put on his oldest clothes, the clothes he hadn't worn since he'd arrived at St. Matthew's. He wanted to be seen as he was before he'd become more like them. The boy from Scranton who knew how to rumble.

He looked up at the dorm windows where now the lights were one by one coming back on, and he saw the boys peering down at him, waiting for the fight to begin. But no one approached or called out to him through the darkness. David stood rooted in the wind and rain, watching for his unseen enemies.

His former friends were also keeping the vigil. Magoo was openly amused, but Chesty, for once, refused to go along with his jokes. Van Kelt and Dillon tried to study. But eventually they, too, put down their books and wandered over to the window, where they were joined by Connors and Reece.

Of all the boys, they were the only ones who knew there would be no fight. They were embarrassed by his straightforward challenge, and none of them was brave enough to confront him.

David waited until the clock in the bell tower began to chime. He counted to eleven as the bells rang out the hour. The wind had risen, and he could hardly see for the curtain of rain in front of his face.

But there was nothing to see. No one was coming. He bellowed into the night. "Cowards!"

* * *

Miss Jones, the Overbrook swimming coach, leaned over the side of the pool and shouted instructions to the girls on the swim team. They raced toward the deep end, churning up the water with their arms and legs. Her whistle shrieked and they changed direction, whipping back to get her critique of their strokes.

But suddenly they weren't paying attention. They were giggling and blushing and looking past her to the entrance of the pool area. Miss Jones turned and found herself face-to-face with a young man who most assuredly did not belong there.

"Yes? May I help you?" she asked the young man.

"Yes, ma'am," he said. "I have to talk to Sally Wheeler."

Miss Jones pursed her lips and glared at Sally, who had the grace to look flustered. But she was already climbing out of the pool and pulling her cap off her head. Miss Jones sighed. Very well, she nodded to Sally. She blew her whistle and resumed the practice.

"What are you doing here?" Sally said in a harsh whisper.

"You wouldn't talk to me on the phone," David said, noticing how her wet bathing suit clung to the curves of her body.

"Sally!" Miss Jones exclaimed. "Would you take your discussion outside?"

"Yes, Miss Jones." Sally grabbed a towel and threw it around her shoulders. Then she hurried outside to the corridor that connected the pool to the rest of the gym.

"Did you *have* to come here?" she demanded.

She wasn't wearing lipstick, her hair was a mess from being stuffed beneath the cap, and water was dripping down her face. But she still looked like a movie star. "Yeah, I had to hear it from you," David said, hardly able to tear his eyes away from her lips.

"You have no idea what I've been through!" She stamped her bare foot on the tile floor. "My mother *died.* She was going on and on. Saying my grandmother would turn over in her grave."

"You could have told me that on the phone," David calmly pointed out.

She shook her head. "My friends are having a cow. Pestering me with stuff like, 'What's it like to kiss a Jew? Does his . . .' " She stopped, too embarrassed to finish the sentence.

"Go on," he prompted her.

" 'Does his *nose* get in the way?' "

He would have thought by now that nothing could hurt him. But he was wrong. "Nice friends," he said.

"At least they're honest. All that stuff about life in Scranton, but you never mentioned the one thing you should have told me. That's not right, David."

"I was afraid you wouldn't want to be with me," he said. He was afraid to ask her the question that was most on his mind, but he had to know. "Would you?"

She tightened the towel around her shoulders. "Please, don't look at me that way. This may come as a big surprise to you, but you're not the first

Jewish boy I ever met. You're just the first who ever denied it."

"I'm the same guy, Sally. . . ."

"I know." Her voice faltered.

He took that as a sign of forgiveness and put out his arms to give her a hug.

"No! I can't!" She shrank away from him. "Not now. You lied to me!"

"I didn't lie to you! I lied to my *father!* I lied to myself!" he angrily protested.

Miss Jones's whistle shrieked a summons.

"I have to get back to practice," she fretted, dropping her gaze.

"Go ahead," he said.

Sally looked up at him, and he saw her eyes were brimming with tears. They stared at each other, and he wished he knew what to say to make it right between them again. But the words wouldn't come. Then she turned and walked away without a backward glance.

Reece had declared a truce. Their friendship wasn't the same as it had been, but David was deeply relieved to have his roommate talking to him again. When Reece suggested they study together for finals, David sensed that he was at least partly forgiven.

After so many weeks of sitting around the table in the common room with six or seven boys, it seemed odd to pair off with only one other guy. But first semester finals were just around the corner, and David was thankful that Reece trusted him enough to be his study partner. French, calculus, chemistry, English . . . Night after night they stayed up late, grilling each other with the questions they thought were most likely to show up on the exams.

Reece propped David up in French and calculus, and David returned the favor in chemistry. They were equally matched in history, and equally daunted by the sheer quantity of names, dates, and facts that had to be memorized. The trick was, David decided, to come up with a system to help them remember all the information. Working from their notes, they made a list on the blackboard of the key events in early British history. They summarized the information with one phrase: WAKE–PAM–RASAF–WARS.

"Which stands for what?" said David, mimicking Mr. Gierash's accent. He picked up a yardstick and pointed to each letter as Reece read aloud the corresponding line.

"William the Conquerer wins the Battle of Hastings.

"Assassination of Becket.

"King John signs Magna Carta.

"Edward the Third claims French throne."

Reece stopped to take a breath, then went on,

"Peasants revolt.

"Act of Supremacy.

"Mary, Queen of Scots beheaded."

They switched places and David took over.

"Roses.

"Austrian Succession.

"Seven Years.

"American independence.

"France."

He sang out the last four letters. "W, A, R, S."

Confident that they were as prepared as they were going to be, the boys smiled and shook hands. They'd earned their right to a good night's sleep.

Van Kelt and Dillon were feeling less secure about the next day's history exam.

"I either know it or I'll never know it." Van Kelt, fully clothed, crawled into bed and muttered, "Sack time."

"You sure your notes are right?" said Dillon, squinting at his roommate's open notebook.

"Yeah." Van Kelt groaned and pulled the pillow over his head to block out the light. "Now all I have to do is remember them."

Dillon peered again at Van Kelt's notebook. He looked over at Van Kelt, whose gently rising and falling body signaled that he was already asleep. He pulled out a small notepad and rapidly copied down Van Kelt's barely legible fact sheet. Then he, too, dropped into bed without getting undressed and fell fast asleep.

Mr. Gierasch's corgi snuffled quietly at the front of the room as his master distributed a question sheet and a blue book to each of the students.

"Please sign your reaffirmation of the honor code in the space provided," Mr. Gierasch reminded them. "This test will comprise thirty percent of your final grade. You may begin."

The boys whipped open their booklets and got to

work. Mr. Gierasch picked up his dog and left the room. The boys were on the honor system. There was no need for him to stand guard to make sure no one cheated.

The only noise in the room was the scratch of pens on paper. David glanced at the bottom of the question sheet and breathed a sigh of relief. The final question read:

PART I. Match the events on the left with the dates on the right.

He thought, WAKE–PAM–RASAF–WARS, and worked backwards, first filling in the blanks on the short answer section:

1. Robert Clive extends British territories in
   India.   I A. 1463
2. Assassination of Thomas Becket.
                                       E B. 1587
3. The British control Suez Canal.
                                       L C. 1666
4. English victory at Crécy.   F D. 1381
5. The Peasants' Revolt.   D E. 1170
6. Mary, Queen of Scots is beheaded.
                                       B F. 1346
7. Duke of Gloucester becomes Richard
   III.   A G. 1611
8. Charles I dissolves Parliament.
                                       K H. 1660
9. Robert Peel repeals the Corn Laws.
                                       J I. 1757
10. Publication of King James Bible.
                                       G J. 1846

Connors was the first to disturb the silence with a loud sneeze, which came out sounding like "Horseshit!"

"God bless you," said Van Kelt.

There was a chorus of shhh's. The interruption broke David's concentration. He looked up and wished he hadn't. Dillon had a small piece of paper cupped in his left hand. He looked at the paper, then scribbled an answer in his blue book.

Lots of kids cheated on exams in Scranton. If you got caught, you were punished. But back home there was no honor code, and Dillon's violation unnerved David more than he might have imagined. He quickly lowered his head and began on the essay questions.

But he wasn't the only boy to catch Dillon consulting his cheat sheet. Van Kelt saw him, too, and hoped no one else had. What was wrong with Dillon? Van Kelt wondered. He was a prefect. He was supposed to know better.

Cursing himself for having looked up at the wrong moment, Van Kelt went back to his exam.

"Time's up, gentlemen," Mr. Gierasch announced forty-five minutes later. "That wasn't so hard, was it?"

The class responded with a chorus of groans. Mr. Gierasch looked around the room and noticed that one of his students still hadn't put down his pen.

"My, my, Mr. Connors," he chided, all but pulling the notebook out from under Connors's hand. "You usually don't have this much to communicate."

"You were bound to ask the right questions sometime, sir," Connors replied cheerfully.

His response brought a chuckle from Mr. Gierasch. "Dismissed, gentlemen," he declared, shooing them out of the room.

Van Kelt was the first one out the door, escaping on his long legs like a startled deer.

"What's with Rip?" said Dillon. "He must have gone down in flames."

"Oh, sure, and I guess you aced it," scoffed Connors.

"Naturally," Dillon drawled.

Connors grunted at his friend's arrogance and punished him with a hip check that sent Dillon's books flying out of his hands. Dillon scowled, hurriedly reclaimed his belongings, and took off after Connors to pay him back.

But he'd missed one piece of paper. Mr. Gierasch saw it as he went to turn off the lights. He bent to pick it up and had to look twice to make sure his eyes weren't failing him. In his thirty years at St. Matthew's he'd never had the misfortune to come upon a crib sheet. It wasn't his eyes that were failing him. It was one of his boys.

After so many hours spent indoors cramming his brain with information David decided he needed to take a longer-than-usual run around the campus. When he finally stopped to rest and catch his breath he found himself leaning against a large boulder to which a bronze plaque had been affixed. He read the plaque aloud:

"THIS TREE PLANTED BY THE STUDENT BODY IN MEMORY OF MARK BOZMAN, 11/4/36–5/25/54."

He was staring at the sapling next to the boulder when Coach McDevitt came up behind him. "Hi," said the coach.

He nodded. "Hi, Coach."

"He wasn't on the team, but a place like this . . . you get to know everybody," said the coach, pointing to the plaque. "Only never good enough, I guess. Nobody saw it coming."

"Whatever he saw, and whatever he didn't see. All the small stuff he sweated, and all the big stuff," said David, thinking more of himself than of the student who was memorialized there. "Who's gonna sweat it now?"

"It's all small stuff, kid."

"I don't think so, Coach. Some of it's pretty big stuff, the kind of stuff you never shake off."

"Greene," the coach said, putting his hand on David's shoulder, "I'm ashamed of all that's happened. I don't know what I expected. That it wouldn't come up, I guess, and if it did, so what? I should have done it different."

"Yeah, me, too." David shrugged philosophically. "But who's gonna know a hundred years from now?"

"Nobody," the coach assured him. "Absolutely nobody."

* * *

The somber expression on Mr. Gierasch's face when he walked into class the next day was the boys' first hint of trouble. Still, his announcement came as a shock to most of them.

"I regret to announce that someone in this class cheated on yesterday's exam," he said.

He held up his hand to quiet the murmurs of disbelief that greeted his revelation. "Everyone signed the honor code. Therefore, we have a rather bleak situation confronting us."

David glanced at Dillon. He, along with the rest of the boys, was watching Mr. Gierasch pace the room. His eyes were still and guarded. Whatever he was thinking remained totally concealed.

"Today is Saturday," Mr. Gierasch continued. "Your next class is on Monday. If the cheater does not come forward or is not identified by then, I will be forced to fail the entire section. Need I remind you what that means?"

Reece's hand immediately shot up. But he didn't wait for Mr. Gierasch to call on him before he spoke. "Isn't that unfair, sir? Only one of us cheated."

"We have all been dishonored by this person, and I will not tolerate it," Mr. Gierasch said firmly.

"How can you be sure someone cheated, sir?" asked David, remembering that the teacher hadn't been in the room during the exam period.

"I prefer to keep the evidence to myself for the time being."

"Can't you throw out the old test and give us another?" Van Kelt suggested.

"Yeah, that's fair," Magoo agreed. "Please, sir . . ."

"And pretend no one cheated? But someone did cheat. Whoever's done this has robbed you of your honor. If I ignore it, he will have robbed me of mine as well." Mr. Gierasch gathered up his materials and marched toward the door. "I leave it in your hands, gentlemen. I don't feel like teaching today."

Nobody moved. The shock of his announcement left the boys angry and grasping for solutions.

"Some son of a bitch better answer," Chesty declared.

"Somebody must have seen something. C'mon, you guys," said Connors.

"Yeah, and do what?" Dillon growled. "Gierasch has dumped it in our laps."

"Great. I work my ass off for four years, and now one lying prick . . ." Chesty hurled his history book at the nearest wall.

"Take it easy, Chesty," said Van Kelt.

Reece stood up and faced the class. "Whoever did this, please, admit it now," he urged. "You can't let him fail the whole class."

"Yeah, you still have time," Dillon said.

"I wish I could get it out of my mind, but I've got this appalling feeling . . ." Magoo was staring in Dillon's direction.

Unbeknownst to each other, David and Van Kelt both nourished the hope that he'd somehow hit upon the answer.

"I have a good idea who did it," Magoo went on.

"Who?" Dillon stared him down.

"Maybe Connors can enlighten us," said Magoo.

All eyes turned on Connors.

"You like having teeth, spastic?" he snarled at Magoo.

"You've been slacking off all term," Magoo shot back. "Hell, Cleary all but accused you of cheating in French."

"Cleary is a sick shit, and so are you, you four-eyed runt! I've been in more trouble than the rest of you put together, but did I ever not admit to something?"

"Okay, so admit to this," Magoo told him.

The words were barely out of his mouth when Connors was vaulting over his desk and going after Magoo. But Chesty and a couple of the other boys held him back in time.

"Get off me!" he yelled. "You pricks are not going to pin this on me!"

He struggled in their grasp until they let him go. He left a trail of curses behind as he stormed out of the room.

"Fine. Just fine," said Reece. "Very cool, Magoo."

"Hey, I'm sorry he's pissed off, but this can ruin the lives of everybody in this room," Magoo defended himself.

"We got three of the prefects here," Chesty pointed out. "You guys gotta handle this."

The other boys voiced their agreement.

"Let's sleep on it and meet tomorrow morning after chapel in the Founders' Room," Van Kelt suggested. "Whoever's guilty, you'd better think about what you're doing."

Once again he left the room in a hurry. This time, however, his roommate caught up with him. Van Kelt decided to make the most of the opportunity.

"What would you do if you knew?" he asked Dillon.

Dillon's response came instantly. "Turn him in."

"Really?"

"That's the code," Dillon said.

He made it sound as if Van Kelt, and not he, needed reminding.

Van Kelt wanted to know how far Dillon would take his deception. "Suppose nobody confesses?"

"Then nobody confesses. Big deal. Gierasch won't do shit."

"He doesn't mess around," Van Kelt disagreed. "He'll fail everybody."

"Believe me, Rip," Dillon said confidently, "the Head's not going to sit still for the failure of an entire section of seniors. Not on your life."

Van Kelt wished he felt as sure of that as Dillon did.

David hadn't been to Dillon's room since Homecoming night. He'd hardly spoken to him since after Thanksgiving, and he would have been happy to avoid him for the rest of the year. He debated pretending he hadn't seen Dillon use the crib sheet. But he'd already suffered the consequences of one lie. He couldn't let another one go by.

He knocked on the door and didn't wait for Dillon to invite him in. "Dillon," he said. "We have to talk."

Dillon turned his back on David and put his feet up on the desk. "We've got nothing to talk about."

"I know it was you."

Dillon picked up his pencil.

"You have to turn yourself in," David said. He waited for some sign that Dillon was listening. "I can describe the crib sheet."

Finally he got a reaction. Dillon swung around to face him but kept his mouth shut.

"That's Gierasch's evidence. Have you seen it since you used it?"

"If I did cheat, and if you did see me and didn't report it, you'd be in violation, too," Dillon pointed out, meanwhile admitting to nothing.

"I know. But I can't let the whole class fail."

Dillon felt the vise tightening. "He's bluffing. He won't fail anybody."

"Gierasch wouldn't bluff."

The stark truth of that statement made a dent in Dillon's defenses. "David, you don't understand the way it is. A thing like this, you don't know what it can do to you. You met my family." He was almost in tears as he appealed to David's compassion. "They expect me to measure up to something that's impossible. I can't do it. I try, but I can't."

David nodded, and Dillon mistook his sympathy for ambivalence. He pressed his advantage. "I'm begging you! All right, I was a prick. I'm sorry. I was a prejudiced prick."

Since that first game they'd played against Winchester Dillon had been begging for special treatment. But he'd never reciprocated with an extra share of understanding when David had needed it. Still, he hadn't come for revenge. "This doesn't have anything to do with that," he told Dillon. "Just confess, okay?"

"All right, goddammit!" Dillon tugged at his tie. He leered at David. "Nothing for nothing, right? How much do you want to keep quiet? Everything has its price. How much will it take?"

David felt almost sickened by Dillon's misreading of his motives. The guy was warped. He couldn't recognize straight talk when it was coming at him like an arrow dead on target. David couldn't bear to be in the room with him anymore. "You tell them or I'll tell them," he said.

"You son of a bitch! Why didn't you stay where you belonged?" Dillon shouted after him.

As Van Kelt had suggested, Mr. Gierasch's students gathered after chapel in the Founders' Room to pin down the guilty party. They soon quit trying to conduct the meeting in any kind of orderly fashion. Everyone was screaming and railing at the unknown culprit. Accusations and counteraccusations ricocheted off the wall like misfired bullets.

Connors was bearing the brunt of the charges. "I guess all I want to know is, how many of you guys think I could have done it?" he demanded of his friends.

Rick, a loud, clownish boy who wasn't privileged to be a member of Connors's group, reminded him, "You did screw up a couple of assignments."

"Yeah?" Connors challenged him. "So?"

"So what're you pulling? C? C plus?" asked Chesty.

"What about this French test we keep hearing about?" demanded Jack, who yearned to be athletic but had to settle for playing trombone in the marching band.

"Cleary said he cheated," Magoo explained.

An anxious Dillon had been keeping a close eye on David. He'd already figured out what he would do if David went through with his threat to turn him in. As soon as he saw David wave his hand to get attention, Dillon jumped to his feet.

"All right, lay off. It wasn't Connors," he said, to David's enormous relief. "This isn't easy for me to say. It's going to disappoint some of you, and I'm sorry about that. I should have told the truth yesterday. I know who cheated. It was Greene."

David did a double take. He couldn't believe what he'd just heard. The rest of the class was equally stunned.

"What?" Van Kelt cried.

"Greene?" yelled Connors.

"Yeah, Greene," Dillon reiterated. "I saw him do it."

"You're a liar!" David jumped up and shouted. "I saw *him* cheat! I told him this morning that I was going to turn him in."

"God, what a squirmer. C'mon, Greene, just admit it," Dillon goaded him.

"I gave him the choice of confessing or . . ." David forced himself to quiet down. "It's not going to work, Dillon."

"I saw him cheat." Dillon held up two fingers, like a Boy Scout. "Word of honor."

"Let's go to Gierasch and tell him the situation," Reece proposed.

"What situation? I turned in the cheater, and he denies it."

"Tell Gierasch," David said.

"Gierasch will just throw it back at us. We have to make the decision," argued Jack.

"Would you both trust us to do what's right?" Chesty queried David and Dillon. "To be fair?"

"Of course I trust the class," Dillon said right away.

Jack turned to David. "Greene? Do you trust us?"

"Why should he trust us?" asked Reece.

"Why shouldn't he trust us? Unless he's got something to hide," Dillon shot back.

"Greene?" said Jack.

"Don't do it, David," Reece warned him.

"What choice do I have? This is the way it's always been done, right?" said David.

"This is the way it's always been done," said Miller, his friend from the dining room.

"Look, do you want to be heard by us or not?" Connors demanded.

"I want to be heard."

"Is that a 'yes'?" asked Chesty.

David took a minute to consider his answer. He was telling the truth. How could that be turned against him? "All right," he said, challenging them to make their system work. "You guys decide."

* * *

The boys agreed that David and Dillon should each be questioned separately by the rest of their classmates. While the students got themselves organized inside the Founders' Room, the two suspects glared at each other from opposite sides of the corridor. Finally Van Kelt appeared in the doorway. "David?" he said.

It seemed so simple. All he had to do was describe exactly what he'd seen. "I was behind his left shoulder. The crib sheet was in his left hand, like this." He demonstrated how Dillon had held the paper. "He'd look at it, then close his hand."

"Why didn't you say something earlier?" asked Magoo.

"In my high school it was called ratting. You don't rat."

"*We* call it being responsible for the standards of the school," Magoo said snidely.

"I guess I thought I owed him something," David admitted, turning it over in his mind. "I was wrong. I should have turned him in."

"Anything else?" asked Van Kelt, desperately hoping David would produce some incontrovertible evidence that would point the finger at Dillon.

"No. It's pretty simple," David concluded. "I saw him cheat, and I didn't do what I should have."

Dillon's story was more elaborate. "I never would have seen him if I hadn't leaned down to scratch my ankle. I just happened to look back when he was opening his hand to check his crib sheet," he explained to the group.

"How come you didn't tell Gierasch or us?" Connors wanted to know.

"I kept expecting him to turn himself in. But considering his previous behavior . . ."

"What 'previous behavior'?" Reece demanded.

"Hey, Reece, everybody knows he's your asshole buddy, but this guy is not one of us, never was. Look, what would you do in my place—all the stuff that happened between me and Greene? I wanted to say something, but I was afraid everybody would say I was just . . . you know, prejudiced."

"That's bullshit! Everybody knows you were doing shit work in history," Reece reminded him. "I wonder how well you did on this test."

"Pretty good, I hope. I studied a lot harder. You guys saw me at the study group. Ask Rip. I was up studying after he hit the sack. Greene needed to pull up his grade as bad as I did. He has to balance out his C in French. And remember, he's not the only athlete applying to Harvard." Dillon resorted to sentiment. "Look, you guys have known me for four years. I'm a prefect, for chrissake."

Hours passed. The students holed up in the Founders' Room weren't any closer to a conclusion than they'd been before they'd heard from David and Dillon.

"Let's face it," Chesty summed up. "It's one guy's word against the other."

Emile, who was a bookworm and seldom spoke up, hesitantly suggested, "Maybe we should tell the Head we can't—"

"We can handle this ourselves," Jack interrupted him. "We've been *told* to."

"Let's just do it!" Magoo urged them. "What's the big deal?"

"Have we heard from everybody?" Reece looked around the room. "Donald?" he asked a tall, bespectacled boy who was prone to stammering.

"I—I s-submit Dillon didn't cheat because he didn't have to cheat. He's . . . he's going to be the f-fifth generation of his f-family at Harvard."

"No one can say that for Greene," Jack reasoned.

"McGivern was supposed to be fifth generation at Princeton," Connors reminded them.

"So?" said Magoo.

"So nothing's for sure."

"What about you, Rip? You haven't said a word so far," said Chesty, realizing that Van Kelt had sat moody and silent all afternoon.

"I'm listening," Van Kelt said shortly.

"Wake up, Rip. How can you think a guy would cheat to get into Harvard when he's already in?" Magoo argued.

"He wasn't in *yet,*" said Connors.

"The only thing I can't figure out is why Dillon waited so long to say something. He's lived with the honor code for years," puzzled Emile.

"That's why he'd be less likely to break it!" Chesty declared.

"But if he saw someone break it," said Emile, "he'd speak up right away."

"Not if it meant he wouldn't be believed because he didn't like Jews," said Chesty.

"Why would *that* bother him?" Reece said, sounding exasperated. "He *doesn't* like Jews!"

"And what are you all of a sudden? A Jew lover?" Magoo sneered.

Reece flopped down on the couch. "I knew it would come down to this."

The "lights out" call could be heard through the door, but nobody moved.

"Let's go over it again," said Keller, a prim-faced boy whose father was one of the ten richest men in America. "As I see it, there's an objective fact. One of them has lied in the past—and one hasn't."

"David never lied about anything," Reece objected.

"Yes, he did," Keller disputed. "He lied about being a Jew. It's not that he *is* a Jew—I don't mind Jews, one of my mother's best friends is a Jew—it's that he *lied* about being one."

"No one ever asked him."

"No one *asked* him because no one had any idea, because he *lied,*" Magoo said.

Van Kelt had left the room earlier to consult with Gierasch. Now he reported, "Gierasch says the crib sheet was block printed. No way to tell who wrote it. He said the reputation of the school and the future of the honor code is on our shoulders."

"S-screw the s-school!" Donald burst out. "W-what about us?"

"Yeah, the school has its honor, and we get our lives ruined," Reece said bitterly.

"My life is screwed if I don't get into Yale!" Jack announced. "I didn't even *apply* anywhere else!"

"I *need* my grades," added Emile. "I'm practically promised a scholarship."

"Same here. No way I can call my father and tell him I failed history," said Jack.

"We busted our butts for four solid years, and now one person is killing us. It's gotta be Greene," Donald concluded.

Van Kelt gave a huge sigh of disgust that caught the boys' attention.

"Rip, what do you honestly think?" Jack said quietly.

"I don't know. But I gotta say it's strange that suddenly this guy is inhuman." Van Kelt shook his head, reluctant to say more. "I mean, what's so different about him anyway?"

"Everything!" Magoo yelled. "Just like my dad says about Jews—from the first minute he was madly trying to ingratiate himself into our crowd. He wanted to get to the top without hazing or any of the work."

"Jesus!" Miller exploded with exasperation. "Can we please keep all that Jewish stuff out of the conversation?"

"We *have* to talk about David being Jewish because he *is* Jewish, stupid," Magoo said condescendingly.

Reece had heard enough from Magoo. "Shut up," he told him. "You're a bigot."

"I goddamn resent that."

"Resent it all you want, asshole. You were the first to start needling him." Reece grabbed Magoo by the shirt and shoved him up against the wall. The other boys were on them in a second, ripping them apart.

"Okay!" yelled Connors, smashing his fist on the table. "I confess."

The room fell instantly silent. Now that Connors had confessed, they were shocked by his admission.

Except he wasn't confessing to being a cheat. "I admit I'm an anti–Semite. I crack Jew jokes. I think they're greedy and pushy, but you wanna know something else? Greene is the first one I ever really knew up close."

"What's your point, Connors?" asked Magoo, straightening his tie.

"That maybe we should think of him before we knew. He was a good guy. A guy who wouldn't cheat."

"This is true," agreed Van Kelt, who was hating himself more as the evening grew later.

"Which means you think Dillon did?" said Magoo.

"Yeah," said Connors. "I think Dillon cheated."

Reese came over to stand next to Connors in a show of solidarity. "That makes two of us."

"Three," said Miller.

"I can't believe this," said Magoo.

"I can't either," said Keller.

Magoo shook his head. "You want to dump Dillon for a dirty Jew."

Dr. Bartram was taking his late evening stroll across campus.

"Good evening, sir," said Mr. Gierasch, passing him from the other direction.

"Good evening, Mr. Gierasch."

He pointed to the light shining through the

windows of the Founders' Room. "Shall I go and remind them of the hour?"

"Let them be," said Dr. Bartram. "I have faith in their judgment."

"It's now one A.M. and ticking. Are we going to decide this or not?" Magoo demanded of the exhausted bunch of boys sprawled across the chairs and couches. Some were already half asleep. Others yawned as they struggled to follow the debate.

"Not if we can't be fair and impartial," said Reece.

"What's the matter with you, Reece?" Chesty asked scornfully. "You know he cheated. We all know what Jews are like."

Reece sat up straight in his chair and pointed his finger at Chesty. "No, I don't! You tell me! What are Jews like?"

"You obviously never met one!" Magoo retorted.

"How many do you know, Magoo?" Miller demanded. "When was the last time a Jew was in your house?"

Magoo hesitated. He couldn't recall that any Jews had ever set foot in his house.

"Tell us or shut your foul mouth!" Miller yelled.

"The only Jews I know are all those commies on the blacklist," Emile announced.

"Are you kidding?" Chesty hooted. "They're all over the place. My dad won't even speak to them."

"I only have to know one." Magoo spewed venom. "The guy that waltzed in here uninvited and pushed himself into Dillon's place on the team."

His comment set off a feeding frenzy of hatred.

"No apology," said Chesty. "Nothing."

"Then he sneaks off with Dillon's girl," said Jack.

"Just like a kike!" Chesty cried.

"Stabbed him in the back!" yelled Emile.

"And he's not even paying his own way!" argued Donald.

"Typical cheap Jew!" Magoo declared.

Reece picked up a chair and threw it across the room. The spiteful chorus went mute.

"You guys want to nail Greene because he knew the way you really feel," he whispered hoarsely into the silence. "Let's not hide the dirty little secrets, guys. Hatred exists. And it exists on this campus, and it exists in this room."

"Is anyone else tired of this?" asked Magoo, clapping his hands to draw their attention. "Let's just vote and get it over with. Hands or secret ballots?"

"Secret ballots!" several of the boys called out.

"I'm against the whole thing, but if we're going to do it, let's at least do it in the open," Reece urged the group.

"Ballots!" shouted everyone but Reece, Connors, and Van Kelt.

The ballots had been counted. David and Dillon were invited back into the room. They stood before the classmates, waiting to hear their judgment.

Van Kelt rose from his seat. His voice quivering with tension, he said, "As head prefect, I've been asked to . . ."

He stopped and watched Reece stand up and stalk out of the room in protest.

"It is the finding of the class—the majority of the class," Van Kelt continued, forcing the words out against his will, "that the guilt lies with David Greene."

Dillon smiled.

Van Kelt's hands shook as he put down the paper from which he'd been reading. "Mr. Greene, you are requested to turn yourself in to the headmaster," he said.

David heard Grandpa's voice in his head, telling him about people who felt so bad about themselves that they needed to blame their troubles on a scapegoat. Only this time David decided he wasn't going to put up his fists and fight back. If they hated him enough to make him their scapegoat, he didn't belong at St. Matthew's. It wasn't the sort of place where he wanted to fit in.

"All right. I'll honor your traditions," he told the boys. "I'll go to the headmaster, and I'll lie."

He took one last early morning run around the campus. A hard frost lay on the ground. The sky was pale, the color of coming snow, and the air had a wintry bite to it. David circled the outer buildings and then did a second loop that brought him to a slight rise overlooking the chapel.

He stood for a moment and inhaled the spicy aroma of the fir trees in the woods just behind him. He thought without regret of all the Christmases that he had never celebrated. Then he turned to survey the campus spread out before him and tried to find a way to say good-bye to all the fantasies he'd spun for himself at St. Matthew's.

He didn't care anymore. He could make his dreams come true no matter where he was. Nor did he care about lying to Dr. Bartram. His classmates had voted him guilty. Nothing he could say would change their minds about him.

The headmaster was waiting for him in his office, along with Mr. Gierasch and the chaplain. Van Kelt was there, too, his long limbs hunched in one of the wingback chairs, looking weary and wan.

"Good morning, Mr. Greene. We were beginning to wonder if you had changed your mind," said Dr. Bartram.

"You know why I'm here?" asked David.

The headmaster nodded. "Indeed. To confess to cheating."

"Yes, that's right," David said, repeating his lines by rote. "I cheated on the history exam."

"You did no such thing," Mr. Gierasch contradicted.

Dr. Bartram gestured to Van Kelt, who leaned forward and spoke in a low, sad voice.

"I saw Dillon cheat." His voice took on a pleading note. "He was my roommate for four years."

"Can I sit down?" David asked, feeling his legs about to give way beneath him.

Dr. Bartram nodded his permission.

David sank into a chair and covered his face with his hands. The swirl of emotions was too great to sort out immediately. But above all he felt relief, and anger, and a tremendous sense of freedom.

"Thank you, Mr. Van Kelt," said Dr. Bartram. "You're excused."

"David, I'm sorry," Van Kelt said feebly before he left the room.

"I *did* break the honor code," David said.

"Yes, as did Van Kelt," Dr. Bartram replied, his face devoid of expression. "But the honor code is a living thing that cannot exist in a vacuum. We absolve you both on that account."

Mr. Pierce walked across the room and put his hand on David's knee, as if to reassure him that he wasn't dreaming. "David, you represent the best of what we hope for at St. Matthew's. Please don't think of leaving," he said, and he shook David's hand.

"Good," Dr. Bartram said briskly. "Then it's settled. I'd like to forget this ever happened."

David stood up and smiled. "No, sir," he disagreed. "You'll never forget it happened. Because I'm going to stay here, and every day you see me, you'll remember it happened. You used me for football. I'll use you to get into Harvard."

He nodded at the three men and left them to discuss their honor code and the future of St. Matthew's.

"I knew we'd have trouble," Dr. Bartram muttered, watching David through his window as he strode jauntily across the campus. "They're a problem wherever they go."

"I can't believe you're suggesting that because we admitted a Jew, Dillon cheated on his exams," exclaimed Mr. Pierce. He glanced at Mr. Gierasch, who shook his head in open disapproval of the headmaster.

"You'll have to excuse me," Mr. Pierce said.

Mr. Gierasch was only one step behind him.

The black Cadillac limousine pulled up next to David as he was passing the chapel. The rear window rolled down, revealing Dillon's presence in the back seat. They stared silently at each other for a moment. Then Dillon said, "You know something? I'm still going to get into Harvard. And in ten years nobody will remember this . . . but you'll still be a fucking Jew."

He seemed oddly serene, as if none of the turmoil had fazed him.

"And you'll still be Grayson Dillon the Third's kid brother," said David, feeling equally calm and resolved.

Dillon's face disappeared behind the smoked glass window, and David walked on. Through the open door of the chapel he could hear the chorus practicing for the Christmas concert.

> Hark the herald angels sing,
> Glory to the newborn king.
> Peace on earth and mercy mild,
> God and sinners reconciled.

Then the bell clock began to chime the hour, and the boys came rushing out of their dorms. David ran to meet them. He didn't want to be late for class.